THE
WHITE
ROOM

USA TODAY BESTSELLING AUTHOR

C.M. ALBERT

THE WHITE ROOM

Genre: Steamy Contemporary Romance

Copyright © 2018 by C.M. Albert | Flower Work Press

Cover by Alivia Anders of White Rabbit Book Design

Book design by Inkstain Design Studio

Editing by Erin Servais of Dot and Dash LLC

How could this book be dedicated to anyone
other than "he who curls my toes"?
This one's for you, babe.

ACKNOWLEDGEMENTS

I'd like to thank my readers, first and foremost. I appreciate each and every one of you. Thanks for sticking by me while I write what my heart feels inspired to and for not being disappointed that I'm so "genre fluid."

As always, so much love and gratitude goes out to my amazing editor, Erin Servais of Dot and Dash LLC. I adore you. You're the best thing I ever found on Twitter. (If there are any remaining mistakes in this book they are entirely my own!)

I'd also like to acknowledge Alivia Anders of White Rabbit Book Design. The White Room would not have existed without your vision, inspiration, and creative genius. Thank you!

Thanks to Nadège Richards of Inkstain Design Studio for the beautiful interior formatting and for the amazing creation of my Limited Edition White Box that was released in conjunction with this book. It was every bit as epic as I dreamed it would be.

Thanks to early readers Sallie, Ellen, and Will, who read my first few chapters and—eh-hem—encouraged me to finish the book already.

Much gratitude to my Colleen's Angels Street Team and Beta Reading Group. They have my back each and every time and are such a positive joy in my life. Many thanks, too, for helping me solve the Henri Basile Bellarose conundrum this time. You're the best.

Biggest hugs to the writers on Facebook who inspire me daily, help me kick it up a notch, or who keep my a** in line: Becky Flade, Beth Michele, Colleen Hoover, Deborah Brown, Desiree DeOrto, Ellen Newhouse, Erin Mandell, Julie Farley, Kenya Moore, Ksenia Anske, Melissa Foster, Michelle Bellon, Nancy Naigle, Nancy Stopper, Shari Slade, Sheila Bliss, Stacy Eaton, Wendy Owens, and Zoe York. Mad love to all of you! Keep being fabulous.

I'd also like to give a nod to the first "steamy" writer I ever read, the Queen of Historical Romance, Bertrice Small (1937–2015). My love affair with epic romance sagas and explicit love scenes started when I was seventeen and my friend Rhonda introduced me to *Skye O'Malley* in the *O'Malley Saga*. No one did it better than Bertrice Small, and I miss her greatly.

Last, and most importantly, my family. Though this is a book I hope my kids never read (or at least until they're thirty!), they and my husband are my everything. I couldn't be more honored to walk through life with such funny, creative, smart, kind humans. Thanks for choosing me.

THE RULES ARE SIMPLE:
NO REAL NAMES.
NO COMMITMENT.
TWO HOURS.

They're put into place to protect us—exclusive
clients lucky enough to afford the cost of playing.

But everyone knows:
some rules are made to be broken.

When hearts and bodies collide,
even the best intentions *slip away* . . .
exposing the true reasons why we
seek the room in the first place.

WILL THE WHITE ROOM
SET YOU FREE? STEP INSIDE
AND FIND YOURSELF.

THE
WHITE
ROOM

CHAPTER 1
DOMINICK

Dominick sat in the pristine white chair as instructed. He could hardly believe he was here, in the land of make-believe. If he'd been asked a week ago, he would've told his buddies it was just an urban legend—one for wet dreams and fantasies.

That was before his best friend, Simon Ellison, handed him a white leather key chain with WR embroidered in silver for his thirty-fifth birthday. He picked up his whiskey and sipped it slowly, the amber liquid sliding down his throat, hot in anticipation.

He had two hours once she arrived. He swallowed hard, loosening his tie, which now felt too tight around his thick throat. He wasn't usually a tie-wearing kind of guy, but in here he could be whomever he wanted. Tonight, he was a confident billionaire executive named Dom. It wasn't exactly original, just a shortened version of his real name—but Dom didn't always play by the rules.

He didn't know who would walk in through the white double doors leading to the suite, but he hoped she liked being spanked and that she would appreciate the two hundred dollars he'd spent on the gray-and-white, Italian silk tie he was now loosening from around his neck. He left it on but let it hang open as his eyes took in the luxurious white space. Across from him was a low, sleek leather couch, in white of course. A white fireplace ran along one wall and was already lit when he'd walked in. Cool travertine tiles surrounded a hearth that rose from plush white carpeting and reached all the way for the ceiling. Everything in the suite was crisp, white, and sterile—a clean slate for anything your imagination could birth. White silk drapes hung on the floor-to-ceiling windows, which were frosted for the privacy they would soon need.

The rules were simple. He'd memorized them as he'd been instructed, the email disappearing from his inbox within ten minutes of opening it.

THE WHITE ROOM

1. Receiving a key to the White Room is by invitation only.

2. The White Room is for adults twenty-one and over. No exceptions.

3. All members are health screened and may not enter without an updated record.

4. You will receive a private line to reserve the room for your pleasure.

5. You cannot make a reservation without your personal, private access code.

6. You may only use the White Room once every six weeks.

7. Men enter the Délice Privé building from Twelfth Avenue using the Beards by Bellarose entrance; women use the Eleventh Avenue entrance next to the Bellarose Spa and Wellness Center.

8. Arrive thirty minutes prior to your appointment.

9. A concierge will direct you to a private waiting room and provide instructions.

10. You have two hours inside the room; a chime will signal when your time is up.

11. Everything must be consensual.

12. No personal information should be exchanged, including real names.

13. What happens in the White Room stays in the White Room.

14. If you break the rules, you will not be invited back.

Despite being a natural-born rule breaker, Dom had no plans to mess up this opportunity. If tonight went as planned, he would be saving up to pay for his next visit in six weeks. He didn't have time for lasting relationships in his personal life, so he hoped this was the answer to his prayers.

A loud click shattered the silence in the room as the double doors swung open. Dom now wished he'd played some music for a little ambiance. The woman who walked in was breathtakingly gorgeous. Long, porcelain legs strode confidently on black high heels that looked runway ready. He stood to greet her, his body a solid wall of muscle hidden beneath his borrowed black suit.

Red. Her lips were cranberry red. Long, loose curls wrapped over one shoulder, her hair so dark and black it shimmered like a raven's wing. He imagined fisting those curls when he yanked her head to his mouth.

Her lips slid slowly into a half-grin, as if knowing where his mind had wandered. Dom groaned as he took in her black garter belt and matching lace push-up bra and panties. She was every inch a lady, and Dom could tell, even without her clothes on, that she was used to having money.

She didn't say anything as she approached him, just studied him with her almond-shaped eyes, heavily lined with black kohl to give the appearance of a cat eye. Dom knew she wouldn't need that much makeup on to be beautiful in her everyday life, but he suspected it was her equivalent of his silk tie: a persona she hid behind while in this room. Soft, but confident. Elegant, but sexy as fuck.

Her eyes never wavered from his on the long walk across the suite's tiled floor. Every click of her heels sent a wave of heat straight to his gut. The confidence of her direct eye contact drove Dom insane with lust. She reached out a hand and placed it on his bicep, squeezing it gently as she trailed her fingers down his well-muscled arm.

"Emmeline," she said, holding her hand out to him.

"Dom," he answered, lifting it to his lips. He pressed his mouth gently to her skin, which was as smooth as his silk tie. He couldn't wait to run his hands over the rest of her body if just her hand was this soft. She smelled clean as if freshly showered, traces of moonflowers clinging to her skin and causing his cock to tighten. "Are you—"

"Shh," she said, pulling his body in toward her with the hand Dom was still holding. "I'd rather not do any talking. We have only two hours together, and I'm starving for the company."

The look in her eyes when she said *starving* was all the invitation he needed. Though how a woman who looked like her could be starving for anything was beyond Dom. But his job wasn't to know about her personal life; it was to worship her for the two hours they had together. And he had every intention of doing just that and not wasting another minute. Dom wrapped his hand around the back of Emmeline's head and pulled it toward him. She purred, obviously fine with a little force.

"I like it a little rough. Is that okay?" Dom growled, staring at her soft, plump lips that she'd painted with precision.

"I like having my hair pulled while being fucked from behind, if that's what you mean by rough," she retorted, her finger trailing to Dom's mouth. She pushed the tip between his lips, her hazel-green eyes never leaving his. He drew in the length of her pointer finger and sucked hard, wishing it were her nipple instead. Her other hand dropped down and rubbed Dom through the outside of his suit pants, his hard length pressing firmly against the warmth of her palm and begging for freedom.

"I'm used to getting my way," he said smoothly after she'd pulled her wet finger from his mouth. "I want to bend you over that boardroom table in the other room and fuck you from behind. I'll pull your hair all you want, as long as I can spank you. Deal?" Dom asked, closing the last inch between them as he cupped her two petite breasts. They were just the right size—plump from the push-up bra, but no more than a perfect handful. Dom slipped his hand behind the lace of her bra and squeezed her nipple hard between two of his fingers, knowing the heat of it would shoot straight between her legs. She pressed her long body up against his in response, just as he'd hoped.

She surprised Dom when she leaned forward and slowly traced the outside of his mouth with her warm, soft tongue. While he hadn't had any qualms about telling her how he wanted to fuck her, he hadn't expected the softness of her tongue or the gentle way she came in for a full kiss. He cupped the back of her head and held her tight, possessing her tongue as they began to engage, slowly at first. He liked the way she wrapped her tongue around his, sucking gently. His cock nearly bounced with anticipation as the pace of their kiss quickened, their tongues plunging deeper as they fought for control.

She chuckled as she pulled back and licked her lips, her eyes piercing his. "Oh, don't worry, your cock will be getting plenty of attention too," she breathed out. "It's one of my favorite things to do."

She grabbed Dom's hand and led him into the other room—what looked like a makeshift boardroom. He watched her delicious-looking butt cheeks flex as she led the way, the black lace teasing Dom over the rise and fall of her twin mounds. He couldn't wait to squeeze them when he pumped into her from behind, knowing they would be supple and yielding beneath the rough calluses of his hands.

The conference room table was long and white and shone to perfection; Dom knew he'd be able to see Emmeline's reflection in it when he bent her over it later. He still couldn't believe he was about to screw a complete stranger. Sure, he'd had his share of women in his earlier years, but most of them he'd known through a friend of a friend. He'd never had an outright one-night stand before, and now he was going to fuck this beautiful woman he'd met just five minutes ago. Strangely enough, he had no issues with that fact, either, and he wasn't sure if that should concern him. For a brief moment, he couldn't help but wonder what her story was and why she was here.

But as she pushed him up against the conference room table, dropped to her knees, and freed his long cock from his pants, he no longer cared. His mind lost all coherent thought as she wrapped her hot red lips around him and began to suck, expertly twisting her hands around his shaft as if she were used to such a wide penis. Oh, this woman knew what she was doing with her mouth, all right. And, goddamn, she was an expert at it. Dom grabbed a handful of black hair and helped guide her head as she drew down on his length and then pulled back up, gently teasing the head with a flick of her tongue.

Dom closed his eyes and groaned. Though he loved the feel of her soft lips around him, he wasn't ready to release just yet, and the woman was relentless with her mouth. Two hours was a long time, and he wanted to go the distance with Emmeline. Even though she seemed more than eager to please him first, Dom wanted to be the one giving. He pulled Emmeline to a standing position, crushing his mouth against hers as their bodies pressed together.

"Did you like that?" he asked, grabbing her ass and pulling her in closer. "Now it's my turn. Sit," he commanded as he lifted her on top of the conference room table. He pulled her hips all the way forward so he had full access to her. He stood between her legs, her wet opening already glistening as it rubbed against his thigh. He pressed his leg against her center as he leaned in for a kiss, her arms wrapping up behind his head. Emmeline's hands rubbed his nearly bald head, brushing lightly over the dark brown stubble that was barely there. In his line of work, Dom needed to keep his hair short—so short a competitor couldn't pull it in the ring.

"God, your head turns me on," she groaned as they lightly nipped each other's lips between kisses.

"Which one?" Dom teased, trailing his mouth along her jawline and down her neck as she continued to rub his scalp. Shivers raced down the length of his body. He never realized how much he enjoyed that simple act.

"Both," she admitted and laughed. "But I've never been with someone who shaved his head before. It's so . . . manly."

Dom chuckled. It wasn't the first time he'd heard that, but her genuine emotion took him by surprise. "Who do you normally fuck, outside of the White Room?" Dom asked, curious.

"My husband," she admitted quietly.

Dom's head snapped up, questioning Emmeline's green eyes. She shook her head, as if disgusted that she'd dropped the veil of fantasy for even a moment. "No more questions. He knows I'm here. Now," she said, pausing as she playfully bit her lower lip, "give me a hot story to go back and share with him," she pleaded, though Dom wasn't sure he believed her. She wasn't wearing a wedding ring. If she wasn't hiding the fact that she had a husband, why take off the ring?

She grabbed his head between her hands and arched into him.

"Suck me," she begged, bringing Dom's head to her chest. He reached up and unclasped her bra, watching as it popped open and her perky breasts rose up to greet him. He'd never seen such pretty nipples before, and couldn't wait to draw one into his mouth. She wanted a hot story . . . he would give her one.

He pushed all thoughts of a husband away and leaned down, tugging one of her perfect pink nipples between his lips. He bit down, rolling the hard bud between his teeth until she moaned, pressing her breast into his face. Dom dropped his other hand between her legs and, sure enough, she was ready for him. "God, you're wet," he groaned. He sucked her nipple all the way in, hard, knowing it would leave a mark.

He trailed kisses down Emmeline's torso, grabbing her waist and pushing her back against the table. She arched off the cold surface, lifting her mons into the air as an invitation. He unclasped the hooks on her garter belt and wrapped his fingers around the outside of her panties to slide them down over her hips. He pulled them down over her black stockings and past her toes. He knew he shouldn't, but he balled them in his fist and shoved them into the pocket of his suit pants before unrolling the thigh-high stockings from her legs.

He looked down at Emmeline, who was now completely exposed on the table in front of him, like an open buffet for his offering. Her sweet pussy was shaved close, what little hair she had left in a neat, narrow strip down the center. If he had to guess, she looked to be around his age, and most women his age tended not to shave themselves down there. It was the younger women he'd dated, the groupies in their twenties, who liked to shave themselves completely. But this was a whole new ball game. He liked the little runway and traced two of his fingers down alongside it, making their way to her warm, wet center. When he gently parted her soft folds and slid two fingers deep inside, she gasped—the sound quickly morphing into something more guttural as he zeroed in on her G-spot.

His fingers danced along her swollen insides until Emmeline was on the brink. Then he slowly removed his fingers and placed them into his mouth, washing away the evidence of her pleasure. She couldn't take her eyes off him as he licked, as if savoring her spicy sweetness. He looked at his watch. They still had an hour and a half. He was going to have some fun. He grabbed one side of his tie and yanked it from his neck. "Sit up," he commanded.

She sat up on the table and looked at him, her body shaking with need and from the absence of his fingers. He wrapped the tie around Emmeline's eyes, securing it behind her head. He hardened even more as he pressed her back against the boardroom table again. This time she was blindfolded and completely at his mercy. "Open yourself for me," Dom commanded.

She parted her thighs, spreading herself on the table for him, completely trusting. He lifted his cock and stroked himself as he looked down at her. God, she was beautiful. Her black hair spread out around her face like some damn princess in a fairy tale. He'd never wanted to fuck someone so badly in all his life. "Play with yourself," Dom said. "I want to see you pleasure yourself before I do."

He watched as she ran her hands down her breasts and over her slender waist, dipping her fingers between her legs as she arched her hips. Using her thumb and pointer finger, she rubbed herself in a familiar, sensual way.

"Slide your fingers inside yourself," Dom rasped as he stroked his long length in rapid movements. Each stroke matched the quick pace of Emmeline's fingers as they slid in and out of her wet opening. "Enough!" Dom was done watching and wanted to taste the source of the sweetness he'd already sampled from his fingers.

He bent over and spread her legs even wider, wrapping them over his shoulders as he plunged his face into her hot center. She was so fucking wet. He licked up one side and down the other, groaning as the muscles in her legs constricted on both sides of his head. He sucked in her nub, loving the gasp she made as her hands flew to his head. Having no real hair to grasp, she held his ears, pushing his head against her in time to the movement of his tongue. He slid his fingers inside as he continued to lick, knowing just how deep to plunge them to get her to soar over the edge. He watched for the telltale signs as her breathing increased, her body bucking to meet his hand.

Soon enough, she started to squirm, the pressure building, becoming torturously unbearable. "Oh my God, Dom. Yes!" she called out as she peaked. He clamped his mouth over her sweet opening as she soared over the edge, her heady taste bathing his tongue.

Dom didn't give her time to recover. He slid her body off the slick, white table and turned her over so she was facedown. He grabbed her long, thick hair into a ponytail and wrapped it around his fist, pulling her head back. Leaning over, he whispered into her ear, "Is this how you like it, Emmeline?" He smacked her ass with his left hand while he gently tugged her hair with his right.

He massaged the red spot where his hand had just left a mark on her beautiful white skin. Dom pressed his hard length against the pliable softness of her ass. "Are you ready to feel me inside you?"

She pressed back against him in response and moaned out, "God yes."

Dom let go of her hair so he could remove his pants and position himself at her warm opening. With one hand clasping her hip, he guided himself slowly inside of Emmeline. She was so fucking tight Dom couldn't help but groan. He slowly moved forward, just an inch at a time, so she could adjust to his width. Finally, he was all the way inside, the tip of his cock nearly bottoming her out. She moaned, throwing her head back as she pushed her rump farther toward him, causing him to brush her even deeper.

He chuckled, wrapping her hair around his fist again and giving it a swift tug. She immediately constricted around him, her body confirming how much she enjoyed that. His cock flared to see such soft hair wrapped around the hard fists he usually used for fighting. He knew he'd never look at his hands and not see her jet-black hair wrapped around them now. *Fuck!*

He slapped her firm butt cheek again and loved when it shook with the impact. She bucked against him when he did, so he began a slow rhythm of pumping inside her while yanking her hair ever so gently. Finally, when he could stand no more of the slow-and-gentle pace, he let go of her hair and grasped both of her hips. He yanked her body toward him and slammed deep inside until she cried out with pleasure. She screamed as he plunged deeper and quicker, their bodies slapping in a frenzied, animalistic rhythm that left them both sweaty and spent.

After feeling her climax for a second time that night, he was finally ready for his own release. "Can I come inside of you?" Dom asked.

"No!" she cried out. "I want to feel you on my skin."

It was enough to unhinge him. He pulled out just in time and released himself onto her lower back. When he was done, he used both hands to rub the warm liquid across her back and around her waist. God, how badly he wanted to slide against her wet body and slip back inside her. He groaned.

"What time is it?" she asked quietly, removing the blindfold from her eyes.

Dom lifted his arm to check the nearly two-thousand-dollar TAG Heuer watch Simon had gifted him with for his last championship belt win. "We have over thirty minutes left. What do you have in mind?"

She turned to face him, rubbing her body against his. "Let's go shower. There's still time to play before our time together is up."

Dom didn't want to think about their time together ending. He held on tightly, pressing her into his heart. He knew what he was getting himself into the moment he'd taken the key from Simon. So why was he suddenly pissed that he wouldn't get to see Emmeline again?

"Hey, no regrets, okay?" she said, taking his hand in hers. She led him from the conference room and into the massive bathroom. They crossed the heated floor and walked over to the white marble shower that took up nearly half the space.

Emmeline ran the water until it became warm enough to step under. She tugged his hand for him to follow her. Dom rinsed his hands and washed himself off before taking her in his arms again. He held her under the multiple showerheads and closed his eyes. It almost felt as if they were standing alone outside in a rainstorm. He ran his hands over her long hair and down her back.

"God, you are so beautiful," Dom told her. "I hope you are told every day how beautiful you are. If you were mine, I'd never let you do this. I would own your body and you would never want another man between your legs. God, what is wrong with your husband, Emmeline?"

She looked up at him beneath the spray, her long, dark eyelashes framing the bright hazel of her eyes. "Don't go there, Dom. You don't know what you're asking, or what you're getting into. You know we aren't allowed to talk about our private lives. It's why I come here. Because I can forget my life at home and be loved again for just a couple hours." She rested her head against his shoulder as they stood there, clutching one another.

"Besides, the next time you visit the White Room, you'll have another beautiful woman in your arms and you'll forget all about me, just as you should."

"How do you know I'll come again?" Dom asked.

"You're too powerful not to," she whispered.

"Can't you arrange to be here again, at the same time as me? I'd love to be with you again, Emme."

"Don't call me that," she said hoarsely. "Please, it's just Emmeline." She straightened in his arms and backed away. "We still have a few minutes. Can I take you in my mouth one more time? I want to be close to you again before I leave."

"There are other ways to be close," he said, nodding in the direction of the giant king-sized bed they could see from the open bathroom door.

"Yes, but I want to taste you, Dom," she said, backing him against the slick, hard surface of the wall. "It's not fair for you to have all the fun."

It didn't seem possible, but Dom grew even harder hearing her say that. Emmeline dropped to her knees and took Dom in her mouth, water streaming over her head and down her long, black tendrils as her head bobbed up and down his shaft. He grasped her hair in both fists and held on as she worked her warm tongue around him, making him gasp with the tight suction she was able to get with her mouth. She cupped him with her free hand, gently rolling his sac between her fingers while her other hand worked his length.

"Emmeline, are you sure you want me to come this way," Dom asked, barely able to hold himself back. She clutched his ass and buried him deeper into her throat in response and Dom lost it. His hips thrust forward and he pushed himself all the way to the back of her mouth. He couldn't help the guttural sound that escaped when he released his seed for the second time in less than an hour.

He pulled Emmeline up and wrapped his arms around her waist, drawing her into his frame like a protective cocoon. "God, Emmeline . . . you are fucking amazing." His body shook from the aftermath of the climax. It had been a long time since he'd come twice in one hour. He quite enjoyed the sensation and wished they had time for a third round.

There were still a dozen things he wanted to try with the adventurous woman he'd just met. They got out of the shower and quickly dried off. Dom slipped his watch back on and checked the time, just in case they had enough for one last quickie.

Damn! How had two hours flown by so fast? There were less than ten minutes left.

"Emmeline—" he began.

She shook her head no as she put on a fluffy white bathrobe that hung on the bathroom door and cinched it tightly around her waist. She quickly picked up her belongings that were scattered around the White Room as Dom forced himself back into the uncomfortable suit he'd arrived in.

"How do we just walk away from each other after that, Emmeline? I'm not usually such a pussy, but that was about as intimate as two people can get. How can I not see you again?"

Dom brushed an errant hair from Emmeline's eyes and tucked it behind her ear as she looked up at him. "You'll get used to it," she whispered, looking away.

Dom swallowed hard, his heart not liking the walls that were slowly being built brick by brick between him and Emmeline. "Have you gotten used to it then?" he asked, not liking the jealous tone that crept into his voice.

"Yes, Dom, I have," she said, searching the room for her panties. "There are rules for a reason, and they're here to keep us safe. Just kiss me one last time before you leave, and believe me when I tell you that our time together was different. Special to me."

Dom studied her face, uncertain whether to believe her or not. He held the back of her head as he lowered his mouth to hers. "I'll never forget you, Emmeline. You were my first in the White Room." Their tongues met, curling around each other's in a moment of shared intimacy that was on borrowed time.

A gentle chime rang out, announcing the end of their time together. As they parted, their eyes met, an unspoken bond passing between them. Emmeline winked at Dom and sashayed from the room, exiting the same door she'd entered just two short hours earlier.

Dom stuck his hand in his pants pocket and grinned as he clutched her panties. He never was one for playing by the rules.

CHAPTER 2
LEXIE

L exie knew the rules. She'd been in the White Room before. Many times. Divorce sucked, but spending her ex-husband's money to live out her fantasies was the sweetest revenge. Served him right for cheating on her—and with his nurse, for God's sake. Could the asshole be any more of a big, fat cliché? She adjusted her peekaboo push-up bra and grinned. Her new ensemble was something he would have begged her to wear during their fifteen years together. Now, someone younger and hotter would get to peel it from her athletic frame.

Her insides tingled in anticipation. The fun part was always waiting to see who would walk through the door. Sure, she'd answered extensive questionnaires about what she liked, whom she was attracted to, and what her boundaries were. But every time was a new adventure, and the six weeks between visits couldn't come soon enough.

She lifted a glass of wine to her lips, enjoying the cool tartness that washed over her now-pierced tongue. It may have taken her thirty-eight years, but the minute the divorce papers were signed, she'd finally gotten her first piercing and first tattoo. She now had three tattoos—the thrill of the needle orgasmic in itself.

She wasn't a bad mother because she wanted these things. She considered it a vital part of her self-care routine. She was finally learning how to make herself happy. And the White Room made her happy.

She paced the room, her leather boots making a sharp clack on the white tile as she walked over to the full-length mirror and ran her hands over her dark brown, five-six frame. The thigh-high boots added a good three inches, and her hair left natural added another two. She loved the gothic chic look she was rocking and how the boots lengthened her legs. It was Victorian meets punk, and was the last thing she ever would've been caught dead in around the other doctors' wives. *God*, Lexie snorted, *if those stuck-up bitches could see me now.*

She still played tennis with a few of them, though many had dropped her like last season's handbag as soon as they heard the D word. Cheating husbands were one thing—everyone in their circle had one—but actually divorcing . . . well, that was another thing all together. Oh well. Lexie pinched her nipples that peeked from the round cutouts in her bra until they stood hard, ready. She couldn't care less what anyone from her social circle was doing right now. All she cared about was who would walk through those white double doors and make her forget.

The door creaked open and in walked a young man in his early twenties. With his sandy blond hair, chiseled abs, and megawatt smile, he looked like he'd stepped right off the pages of an Abercrombie & Fitch advertisement. His teeth were whiter than the room, and dimples flanked the sides of his perfectly sculpted mouth. *Dear God*, Lexie thought, *if my panties had a crotch, they'd be drenched already.*

He walked over, his head down, his blue eyes gazing up at her— all Justin Bieber innocent like. *Yeah, he has an M.O., and he knows he's hotter than sin.* When he reached her, he cupped her chin and dragged his gaze slowly from her stiletto boots all the way up to her eyes. She was wary when he leaned in close and whispered, "I have a surprise for you."

He pinched one of her pert nipples and grinned. *Damn. He is almost—almost—too adorable to fuck.* Lexie was used to being the one in control and didn't like that he had a surprise. Especially being as young as he was. She reached down and cupped his balls through his jeans. "I'm the one who's in charge in this room, do you understand me?"

Lexie was used to having her submissive partners obey her the moment they walked in through the door—or crawled. She'd said she'd be open to playing a sub just once, but this young man didn't look emotionally strong enough to dominate her.

"It's not that fantasy," he said, bringing his mouth just inches from hers. He ran his tongue over Lexie's plump bottom lip. "But I was told there was something I could do that you would like." He ran his hand down Lexie's arm, over the black lace glove she was wearing. She shivered in excitement.

Okay, so maybe an element of surprise *was* what she needed.

"What do you have in mind?" she purred. She ran her hand over his chiseled chest, straight toward the hard V-line of his groin. And this—this was why she loved younger men. They would be fucking the entire two hours.

She was surprised when the door opened again and a beautiful, raven-haired goddess glided in. She was completely naked, save for her long black curls that covered the tops of her gorgeous tits. Lexie swallowed, hard. She'd been coming to the White Room for a long time now, and never once had they delivered on this fantasy for her. She'd almost forgotten that she'd approved it.

"Ah . . . this is Emmeline," the young man said, though his eyes never left the woman who walked toward Lexie. It was as if he'd been just as surprised as she was at who walked in. "And I'm Asher," he said, quickly recovering.

The woman stopped in front of Lexie, incredibly close in her personal space; though, all things considered, they were about to be all up in each other's business.

"Well hello," Emmeline said, those two simple words coming out throaty and sexy as hell.

"Hey," Lexie whispered back. Gone was the leather-wearing dominatrix Lexie thought she was walking in as tonight. She glanced between Emmeline and Asher, uncertain of who would be the one in charge. The uncertainty unnerved her. Ever since the divorce, Lexie wasn't a fan of relinquishing control. She always said she'd never do it again. *Damn!*

"We don't have a lot of time," Emmeline said. "You are comfortable with this arrangement, aren't you?"

Lexie nodded. "Of course," she answered in a low, husky tone. "It just surprised me. Are either of you submissives?"

They both shook their heads no.

"Well, fuck," Lexie breathed out.

Asher laughed and grabbed her hand. "What's your name tonight, gorgeous?"

"Lexie."

"Come with us to the bedroom, Lexie. Emmeline and I have both had threesomes before, though never with each other, of course." He glanced quickly at Emmeline, then returned his attention to Lexie. "But we were both briefed by our concierge."

"Must be nice," Lexie retorted. She followed behind Asher, enjoying the feel of his strong hand grasping hers. Her eyes stayed glued to his broad back as his muscles flexed and shifted. His skin was smooth and flawless, not a hair in sight. Another reason she loved younger men: no unsightly body hair.

They stopped in front of the bed, and Lexie sighed when a soft pair of arms circled her waist. Emmeline's kisses started at her shoulder and found their way into the crevice of her neck. She'd never kissed a woman before—or been kissed by one—but Emmeline's lips were every bit as soft as Lexie imagined them to be. She closed her eyes and succumbed to the sensation of soft butterfly kisses on her back as Emmeline's hands trailed lightly down her sides to her hips. Her lips found their way to the small of Lexie's back and sucked gently, sending waves of pleasure over her body. She gasped out loud when another set of warm lips closed over one of her nipples, a large, firm hand massaging her other breast at the same time.

Yes! She'd let them both be in charge! Lexie sighed, giving over to the hedonistic pleasure of being touched by two sets of hands at once. Asher's mouth was surprisingly aggressive for such a pretty boy, and the sharp contrast between his teeth tugging at her hard, brown nipple and the light brushes of Emmeline's lips along the low of her back nearly unraveled Lexie.

Her body moved on its own accord. She found herself swaying against Asher as he pulled her in close and dropped his mouth to hers. His tongue dove straight in and danced with hers in the most symbiotic way. His hands were on her breasts the entire time, rubbing them, worshipping them with a tight tug and pull of his fingers. Emmeline slid her naked body up, rubbing against her back. The woman's taut nipples brushed across her skin as those full lips found Lexie's neck again.

Lexie moaned as she leaned back against Emmeline, the woman's fingers dancing their way across her stomach and down to her crotchless panties. She felt Asher's teeth clamp down roughly on one of her nipples, just as the tip of Emmeline's manicured nail circled and teased her clitoris. Lexie knew she'd be a hot mess before they ever made it to the bed. She hadn't anticipated how much the excitement alone would send her over the edge. She lifted her hands and brought them to the sides of Asher's head, following it as he brought his mouth and that warm, wide tongue of his all the way down her abdomen to where Emmeline was busy rubbing Lexie's sensitive little nub from behind.

Asher dropped to his knees and leaned in, slowly flicking her sex with his tongue. Lexie kept her hands in Asher's hair and massaged his head as he leaned in farther and took hold of her clit in his warm, wet mouth. She gasped when Emmeline's hands cupped her ass and she began sucking on one of her firm, round cheeks. Emmeline's capable fingers massaged the muscle as she licked the surface completely. The feel of the woman's small tongue on her backside, while Asher's head dipped between her legs on her front side, was more intense than almost anything Lexie had ever done—

and she had done a lot during her times in the White Room. But there was something so sexy, so on the edge of reason, to feel two tongues taking her at the same time in such a vulnerable way.

"Come here," Asher growled. He stood and removed his jeans, climbing on the bed in all his naked glory. He was hard and ready, but Lexie had been enjoying his tongue on her and was hoping he'd finish what he started. He reclined fully, crooking a finger for her to join him. Emmeline stood, taking her hand and leading Lexie to the bed so they could climb on together. For the first time, she was at a loss. They were both so beautiful, and she wasn't sure whom she wanted to touch first.

Asher solved that quickly for her. "I'm not done with you yet, princess. Get up here."

No one had ever called her *princess* before. Especially a man younger than she was. She was beginning to suspect Asher wasn't all just innocent dimples and flat abs as she'd first suspected.

"That's right, you're not done with me yet," she said, crawling up the bed on her knees. "I want to feel that deliciously wide tongue of yours all the way up inside me. Can you do that for me, pretty boy?" she teased, tweaking her nipples as she met Asher's bright blue eyes.

"It's what I wanted the minute I walked in here, Lexie," he growled, surprising her. "Now get up here and sit on my face."

Lexie couldn't imagine being any wetter than she was at that moment. Until he said, "But you are to face Emmeline, because I want her to suck your beautiful tits while she rides me."

Lexie wasted no time turning around and sliding over Asher's mouth. He reached both hands up and covered her thighs, pulling her down onto his face. She cried out in pleasure as his nose slid up and down her wet opening. Emmeline bent down, cupping Asher's sac as she took the long length of him in her mouth, sliding all the way down to his base in one fluid movement. Asher made low animal noises in response, though his mouth never left Lexie.

Instead, he used that heat to lash out as Lexie rode his face. The stronger his hips thrust to meet Emmeline's demanding mouth, the farther Asher's tongue rose to ravage the depths of Lexie's hot center. His nails dug into her butt cheeks as he held her down, increasing his rapid pace. Her eyes met Emmeline's as the woman flicked her tongue back and forth over the opening at the tip of Asher's cock, teasing him gently. Lexie was this close to coming when Emmeline deftly swung her leg over his body, letting her bottom sink inch by inch down Asher's impressive length, her eyes never leaving Lexie's.

It was too much. Lexie closed her eyes and swayed her body faster over Asher's mouth. Just when she needed relief the most, he thrust two of his long fingers deep inside and pistoned them back and forth. Her insides contracted and released when Emmeline leaned over and bit down sharply on her nipple, her tongue easing the pain away. White bursts of light exploded behind Lexie's eyelids as she climaxed, releasing her sweet juices all over Asher's mouth.

His tongue never stopped licking as her body spasmed, slowly riding down the wave of her intense orgasm.

Time stood still as Lexie regained her senses, coming back to her body after experiencing the nirvana that was Asher's mouth. She lay next to him on the bed, thoroughly enjoying the sight of dark-haired, fair-skinned Emmeline trotting up and down on his cock in a steady rhythm, riding him cowgirl style. She longed to reach out and touch her, but she didn't want to impede Emmeline's orgasm. Instead, she rolled over and kissed Asher's chest, taking one of his nipples in her mouth. What she wouldn't do for a nice pair of nipple clamps right now.

His arm wrapped around her and he pulled her closer so they were eye to eye. Asher took her tongue deep in his mouth and sucked hard, sending ripples of pleasure between her legs. She could taste herself on his breath as he sucked on her tongue. She wished to God she was the one riding him, the one who was about to make him come.

As Emmeline rubbed her clit faster, Asher forced his hips up, slamming into her as her bottom crashed down against his flat stomach. They rode each other like this, Asher's hands steadying Emmeline's hips so he could push up even farther. Even though Asher had licked her clean, Lexie could feel herself getting wet all over again as Emmeline's head fell back, her hips grinding down as she released. Her body was still shaking from her orgasm when Asher bellowed out, thrusting one last time as he took his own pleasure.

Emmeline's chest rose and fell as she collected herself, slowly opening her sexy hazel eyes. They were still half clouded with lust when she pinned Lexie with her heated gaze. "We still have time, let's go get clean."

Lexie followed Emmeline to the bathroom, where she quickly turned on the shower. Asher was right behind them. Her heart raced with anticipation, even though she already felt as if her night was complete. Lexie quickly unzipped her boots and slid her panties off. She was the only one still partially dressed.

Emmeline peeled Lexie's black lace gloves off, holding her hand as they stepped under the cool spray of water together. She guided Lexie to sit on the built-in bench, and the cold, wet marble sent a trail of goose bumps racing up her arms. Asher joined them and quickly rinsed off as Emmeline soaped up a washcloth. She bent down, running the soft cotton back and forth over Lexie's wet center, causing her to spread her legs open wider. Asher walked over, lifting her chin so their eyes locked. "Your turn, princess," he said, holding his cock out to her.

The small fibers of the washcloth sent tiny sparks of heat directly to her core—her insides melting as Emmeline's sudsed-up body slid between her legs. Lexie opened her mouth to receive Asher and nearly choked when he deftly pushed his way to the back of her throat. He was much larger than she'd guessed. She took both of her hands and wrapped them around his shaft, twisting as she sucked on

30

him. She moaned when a nimble pair of fingers parted her soft folds below. Lexie swayed her hips, meeting Emmeline's palm as it moved back and forth against her mons, her fingers dancing deep inside.

Lexie quickened her pace to match the one Emmeline was setting; when Emmeline slowed, Lexie slowed. As she got comfortable with his size and their pace, Lexie reached around and grabbed Asher's ass, pulling him in as far as he could go. He groaned, lifted one leg up on the bench, and held her head as he pumped faster into her mouth. Lexie knew he was on the brink of climaxing, just as she was, so it surprised her when Asher pulled out and stroked himself slowly.

"Don't take your eyes off me," he commanded. "Even as you come."

Lexie gasped when Emmeline slid a third finger deep inside her, her mouth drawing in one of her hard, brown nipples and latching on. She kept eye contact with Asher while Emmeline's hand stayed busy below, her fingers quickly finding her G-spot. The sensation of Emmeline's teeth scraping against her sensitive nub while Asher pinned her with his ocean blue eyes pushed Lexie up higher and higher until she could hold it no more and sailed right over the edge. Her insides shook as she tried to maintain eye contact, but it was impossible. Lexie closed her eyes at the last moment, her body rolling in sync with Emmeline's hand as she rode her orgasm to completion.

Man, she felt alive!

When Lexie finally opened her eyes, Asher still had her pinned with his intense gaze. "Naughty girl," he said. "You failed to keep your eyes open."

Lexie's insides clenched, her body still buzzing with sensitivity. Emmeline helped her up before running her sudsy hands over Lexie's body. "Let's get clean," she said, glancing at Asher. "We may still have time for one more round, and by the look in his eyes, he's not through with you yet." Emmeline slid her hand between Lexie's shaky legs, the hard ridge sliding right down the center. She leaned forward and whispered, "Neither am I."

Holy hell. Lexie didn't know if she had one more round in her, but the pulses of heat that shot between her legs told her she probably did.

Emmeline brought her lips to Lexie's. Despite all the intimacy they'd shared, this was the first mouth kiss between them. It felt even more vulnerable than anything she'd done with Emmeline so far. The woman tugged at her generous lower lip, biting it gently. Her tongue was as soft in her mouth as it had been on her pussy.

Lexie moaned when Emmeline backed up against the wall and pulled Lexie with her, drawing her in so close their bodies melted together. The thrill of not being in charge and not knowing what was coming next left Lexie feeling high, untethered. The women slid their soapy bodies against one another as they stood under the cool spray. Lexie's hands found Emmeline's small, but perfect, tits and held them. She wanted so badly to suck on one, but she'd never done that before. It was different having it done to her than doing it for someone else. Emmeline saw her struggle and helped her, winding her hands in Lexie's soft curls and lowering her head to her breast. Lexie darted out her tongue, just as she did on Asher's chest. Except this time, her tongue found solace on the hardest, sweetest nipple she'd ever tasted. Her mouth covered Emmeline's areola easily, and she began sucking, rolling her tongue around the woman's sensitive bud. It made Lexie think about Emmeline's other sensitive bud and if she'd have the courage to taste it, too.

She knew she had to find out. This might be her only chance. She left a wet trail of kisses down Emmeline's pale skin as she lowered to her knees. When she looked up, Emmeline's eyes were half-closed in heated anticipation. Her hands pressed firmly into the wall behind her as she arched her hips forward, inviting Lexie to taste her.

Lexie closed her eyes and went on instinct, lowering her kisses to the woman's stomach, the curve of her upper thigh. She thought about what she liked and did the same, taking one long, slow lick up her glistening center and latching onto her sensitive spot. Emmeline's body shook in appreciation and Lexie grew hot knowing she had that kind of power over another woman.

She held onto Emmeline's outer thighs and leaned in, flicking her clitoris with her tongue. Emmeline's hands tightened in Lexie's hair, encouraging her to keep going. This time when she lapped at the woman's slick opening, she found it even wetter, more swollen. She parted the soft folds before her and arched her tongue inside, exploring the sweet stickiness she found.

Lexie discovered she rather enjoyed Emmeline's spicy flavor. She used her nose as Asher had earlier and dragged it up and down, taking a moment to rub it at the top while her tongue lapped inside. She kept up this pattern of lick, slide, suck, lick slide, suck until Asher's hands wrapped around her waist.

His mouth was hot on her neck as his hands slid down her slick body and grabbed her tight ass. He leaned forward and growled in her ear. "Get on your hands while you lick her," he instructed.

Lexie was panting with desire as she set her hands down on the cold marble tiles, lifting her head to explore Emmeline's sweet pussy again. Now a little lower, she was able to maneuver her tongue all the way up inside. Emmeline bucked against her face, and soon Lexie wasn't sure if she was moving to lick her or if Emmeline was sliding across her mouth. It didn't matter; she just wanted to keep tasting Emmeline's intoxicating flavor.

As she licked, Asher slid into her from behind with no warning, filling her full. He wrapped his hands around Lexie's little waist and slowly pistoned in and out. He barely put the tip back in, teasing her hot center. Lexie pushed back, needing to feel that hardness inside her again. Asher let her slide her bottom back, taking him in all the way. When she had reached the end, her bottom slapping his stomach, he held her there, not letting her move. He hiked one leg up and began to make small circles with his hips, hitting her insides in all the right places.

"Yes," she panted, pushing against him for even more.

He grabbed Lexie's hair, tugging her head back. "Liked that, did you, Lexie?" he asked, breathing heavily into her ear from behind.

"Oh, God. Yes," she moaned.

He pulled back again, almost all the way out.

"No!" she cried, trying to push herself back down his cock again.

"Uh-uh," he said, holding her hips firm. "This is what you get for closing your eyes on me, naughty girl. Lick her," he commanded, doing tiny little pistons in and out of her with just the tip of his cock. Lexie wanted to scream at him to fuck her already!

But she leaned forward and pushed her tongue back inside Emmeline, lapping her way up one side and down the other.

Slam! Asher had gripped Lexie's hips and bottomed her out in one swift movement. She saw stars and moaned, her mouth still latched onto Emmeline.

He pulled out and flipped Lexie over, almost knocking the wind out of her as he lay her back against the cold, white tile. "Eat her pussy," he commanded, "and don't stop until she comes."

Emmeline dropped to her knees over Lexie's head and lowered herself to her eager mouth. Lexie pushed her fingers inside the woman and worked them back and forth until she found a steady rhythm. Just when she had it down, Asher lifted Lexie's hips and slid inside her. It wasn't long before his long cock was rocking her body back and forth across the cold tiles, her own body screaming for release.

Emmeline slid her torso back and forth over Lexie's mouth at a feverish pace, Lexie's nose pushing against her sensitive clit with each pass. Emmeline reached down and held Lexie's head between her hands as she slid back and forth, her thighs finally tightening around Lexie's face as she came.

That's when Asher spread Lexie's legs wide apart and plunged deep inside of her, his arms holding his torso above her as he looked down into her stormy blue eyes. "Now you get your release," he promised as he pulled back, then slammed back inside her.

Water fell all around them as he slid back and forth, holding nothing back this time. His body glided easily against Lexie's slick torso as he rocked his pelvis, slamming deep inside her over and over again—nearly pushing her head to the wall in his exuberance. "I want you to come with me," he grunted. "Are you close?"

Lexie could hardly answer as her insides clenched, hot and swollen around Asher. "I'm there," she screamed, bucking up against him as she came. Asher buried himself deep inside Lexie for a few quick thrusts until he exploded too, sinking even deeper as he came.

Lexie lay spent, her body deliciously sore and tired. Asher helped her to her feet, led her to the water. Their bodies were shaking as they all leaned back against the shower walls, spent. Emmeline turned the spray to hot as they rinsed the passion from their bodies. It was if they were scalding away the images of their three bodies writhing on the shower floor—though Lexie knew she didn't ever want to forget.

She was sad when they were dressed and the quiet bell chimed, signaling their time was over. Lexie knew she'd never see either of them again, but she wanted to thank them. For the first time since her divorce, she'd finally felt in control again, and not just by causing someone else pain. She realized she'd been taking out her hurt on the wrong people.

She realized that being in control and having power came from being vulnerable just as sure as it came from being the one in command. A sense of freedom washed over Lexie as she walked from the White Room, leaving Asher and Emmeline behind.

She was confident now that she could both control and lose control, and she knew she was safe either way.

CHAPTER 3
ASHER

Of all the fantasies Asher liked best, Mrs. Robinson topped his list. Older women were just more confident. They knew what drove him insane and they appreciated his stamina, often matching it pace for pace. Besides that, they were much raunchier and experienced than women his own age. Quite frankly, he had bored of them and rarely dated anyone in his peer group anymore. From time to time he did, just to keep up appearances. But the White Room had been his sanctuary and freedom these past four years since graduating college. When the demands of law school had pressed firmly on his chest, he appreciated the release this gave him. And the bonus? No one his age could afford it, so his secret was safely confined within these walls. Yeah . . . he knew it was a dangerous path to walk, given his profession, but the temptation of the room was too much—especially after getting his first taste four years ago as a college graduation gift from his father.

Most dads bought their sons an expensive vacation or a sports car for graduating top of the class from an Ivy League school. Asher snorted. Not his dad. His dad passed on the family legacy—VIP access to the White Room. As a founding investor and part owner, Mr. Wells and all five of his sons had unlimited lifetime access to the White Room. Every day, if they wanted. Of course, no one could fuck that much. Not even Asher, and he was one of the randiest of the five Wells brothers.

The White Room had been his escape from the grind of law school, from the demands of an overbearing father, and from the day-to-day monotony of life after school. After this visit, he wasn't sure how frequently he would be able to visit though, as his career—and his father—were pushing a move on him that Asher wasn't sure he wanted. Oh, he knew he'd still fly back for visits. After all, it wasn't every day a young man with a perpetual hard-on could live out any and all fantasies his mind could create. It would be difficult to find a woman to match his lust, stamina, and creativity—outside of the White Room, that was.

He sat in the white leather chair and slowly stroked the outline of his cock in a pair of pastel pink, flat-fronted linen trousers. Today he was dressed as if it were just another day at the Kentucky Derby, as he was fulfilling a fantasy for someone else. He loosened his baby blue tie that matched his eyes and stood to shrug off his dark navy sports jacket when the door opened.

A woman in a long, flowing coral sundress walked in confidently, her copper-colored hair swung over one shoulder in a long, loose, complicated braid. She wore a wide brim sun hat that matched, shielding her eyes from Asher. That was okay, because he couldn't look away from the long, thin legs that parted the sundress as she walked, playing peekaboo with the treasures he imagined that lie beneath the folds of silk cloth.

She stood in front of him and grabbed onto his tie, still not lifting her head or showing him who was beneath the wide brim of the tan and coral sunhat. "You're the perfect boy for a day at the races. You'll do quite nicely. Do you have a horse in this race, young man?" She nearly purred as she slid her long, manicured coral nails up and down his tie suggestively.

"Yes, ma'am. I only breed and race stallions. Mine is a champion."

"I bet it is." She chuckled lightly, pulling Asher in closer by the tie. "You aren't too young to race, are you? My men seem to be getting younger and younger every time—not that I'm complaining. The races always last longer with younger jockeys."

Asher lifted her up in one swift movement and flung her partially over his back, walking her over to the long, white leather sofa. He set her down right in the middle, gently pulling her legs forward so she slid down against the low back, her head resting perfectly on its ridge. That's when he noticed her dark black Jackie O sunglasses that completely covered her eyes. "Take them off so I can see you," Asher commanded, reaching out his hand. She shook her head no, sending ripples of frustration through his body. He liked looking into the eyes of the women he fucked. But if she needed anonymity, she would have it.

For now.

"Fine, have it your way," he said. "But make no mistake, I'll not go easy on you just because you hide. I'll fuck you so hard those sunglasses won't stand a chance of staying on that gorgeous face of yours. Besides, they're just going to get in the way when you wrap those beautiful coral lips around me."

Asher burned hot when her face flushed pink. Her hands flitted to the long double strand of pearls around her neck. Asher couldn't wait to see her in nothing but those beads. He took a deep breath and focused on the woman's chest. She was playing a big game, but Asher could tell by the rapid pulse of her breathing that, despite her age, she was a novice to the White Room and he needed to pace himself.

Asher dropped to his knees in front of her and gently slid her legs apart, slow and deliberate. He pushed handfuls of silk up her legs and around her waist on the cold white couch. Goose bumps raced up her legs when he placed his warm hands on either side of her outer thighs and inched them up slowly, patiently. He watched as her breathing hitched and noticed there was something about the familiar shape of her mouth as she parted it, her hands still playing with the cool, white pearls around her throat.

"What's your name?" Asher asked, not that it mattered. Everyone used fake names in here. Everyone except him. It was part of the thrill—a big fuck you to the man.

"You can call me Wendy," she said.

"Wendy, huh? You like lost boys, then?" Asher teased, sliding his hands between her thighs and parting them, delighted at the exposed red curls his fingers brushed against. "You won't feel lonely with me, Wendy. I'll be your Neverland."

She gasped when his fingers found her sensitive nub, sliding slowly up and down the front of her folds, gently working them apart. Asher leaned forward and was just inches from Wendy's mouth. He cupped her face with his left hand, while his right hand delicately traced the outside of her sex, trailing up and down her inner thigh, and back to center. He loved the way she squirmed beneath his touch. He could tell she was dying to press into his hand and invite his fingers inside of her. But he was going to take this slow. Even though she was older—the Mrs. Robinson he'd been hoping for—it seemed as if he was going to be setting the pace, not the other way around.

"So . . . Wendy. What brought you to the races today? A little escape from reality?" he asked, gently pushing the folds of her outer lips apart with his fingers, while his mouth moved closer to hers.

Those damn glasses were already getting in the way, and he wanted to taste those plump, coral lips. Wanted to see how sweet she really was beneath the pearls and three-hundred-dollar designer sunglasses.

"One. Last. Time," he snarled, sliding his finger deep inside her as he ran his tongue slowly along her bottom lip. She jumped beneath his touch, her body shuddering with anticipation. "Take the glasses off."

A little moan escaped her lips as they parted, and she lifted ever so slightly for his mouth. He pulled back, using the hand that he'd held her face with to slide his thumb toward her waiting mouth. "Are you sure you're ready for the pace I'll be setting in today's race?" he asked, sliding his thumb slowly inside the corner of her mouth.

She sucked on his finger, pressing her chest toward him. She was small beneath the sundress, so small she didn't need a bra. Despite having about twenty years on him, her breasts were firm, high, and round. Her mouth told him she wasn't as innocent as she was pretending to be, so why was she hiding?

He pulled his thumb from her mouth and removed his finger from within her sweet, wet folds beneath her skirt. He reached his hands up slowly toward her sunglasses and whispered, "I'm going to remove these now, Wendy, so I can see you when I take you. I need you to let go of your outside life and trust me. Can you do that?"

This time she nodded. She reached her hands up and covered Asher's fingers over the arms of the sunglasses. "You will recognize me," she whispered. "Please don't leave when you do."

Together they slid the sunglasses from her face. She did look familiar, but Asher couldn't place her right away. In his social circle, it wasn't uncommon to be surrounded by beautiful older women— they seemed to flock around his father. "You don't recognize me, do you?" she asked as she let out a shaky breath. "That's good actually."

Asher watched the way her lips formed their words, saw the delicate splash of freckles against her chest. He ran his eyes up her chin and to the small mole on the upper part of her lip, toward the corner. He'd seen that before . . . he just couldn't place it. Then his eyes met hers, recognition slamming into his gut. She smiled shyly, knowing he'd placed her.

"Vironica Mason," he said slowly. His gaze never left hers, taking in the vibrancy of her kelly green eyes rimmed with laugh lines that crinkled when she allowed herself to smile. He wanted to see more of those lines. Her eyes lit up when she smiled. Her lips were full and her mouth was wide, something he'd never paid much attention to until now.

"This doesn't have to be awkward," Asher said, running his hands along her thighs again. "I'm no longer Katie's high school friend. I've been to college, graduated top of my class. Went to law school, and am a practicing lawyer now. I may be younger in age, but

I promise I make up for it in experience. This isn't my first rodeo, Mrs. Mason. I come here to please, and I promise you I will."

Her eyes moved toward his mouth, focusing on his lips. "My husband died, you know. I've only been here a few times. Your father suggested it, in fact. He was a good friend of Tommy's, though Tommy never came here, of course," she clarified.

"It doesn't matter. That's the whole point, isn't it? Today you're just Wendy. You don't have to be anyone else, anywhere else. It's just you, me, and the Kentucky Derby," Asher said, his mouth lifting into a seductive smile he knew worked. "Care for a ride?"

She nodded, this time finding her voice. "But first, I'd like you to keep doing what you were before . . . with your fingers."

"Lie back then, darling," he growled, pushing her against the low back of the sofa. Her head relaxed back as soon as he slid his finger back inside her. She let out a slow moan, this time arching her hips forward to meet his hand. She'd been nervous because she'd recognized him from their social circle. But now that she was free to just be herself, Asher had a feeling her inner Mrs. Robinson would come out to play—and he couldn't wait.

He dropped his head and kissed the small hollow part of her clavicle. She gasped as he ran his warm tongue over her pebbled flesh. His finger continued to slide in and out, her slick juices making each motion a little easier. Asher trailed his kisses down her chest, easily sliding the thin straps of the sundress over her petite shoulders. They pooled down her arms and her small breasts were free for him.

He dipped his head and took one of her dark pink areolas in his mouth. They were big, considering the size of her small tits, and the tight, large nub of her nipple was like a small pacifier in his mouth. He sucked greedily, pulling in a large section of her breast too. His hand found its way down her small waist and to her pooled dress that was still hitched up around her waist on the sofa.

"Stand for me, Wendy," he commanded. Her sundress dropped to the ground and Asher took in the shape and delicate curves of her body as she stood before him, completely bare except for her long double strand of pearls. "My God, you are beautiful."

Vironica stepped out of her sundress and kicked it gently to the side. She ran her hands down her chest, over her pert breasts, and to her stomach. It was slightly curved from the birth of her daughter, but she was trim, fit for her age. Her legs were long, and made to look longer in her high-heeled wedge sandals with complicated straps running up her taut calf muscles.

"Dear God, please leave those on," Asher said, pulling her close. "Those, the pearls, and that fucking sexy braid are going to give way to many fantasies long after today," he growled.

Her lips curved into a knowing smile. "A woman has to have a secret weapon or two," she murmured. "But one of us is overdressed," she said, wetting her mouth with her soft pink tongue as it slid over her full lips.

She tugged at Asher's baby blue tie, loosening it and sliding it out from under the starched white collar of his button-up shirt. "Don't you look adorable in your derby finest," she said, eyeing his frame appreciatively. "You come from good stock."

She smoothed her fingers up and down his biceps after she dropped his tie to the sofa. He leaned over to pick it up. "Not so fast, Wendy. I have something in mind for this."

She rubbed her naked body against him and shivered. "Tell me what you want to do with it," she whispered before finding his mouth. She bit playfully at his lower lip, her hands trailing up the hard muscles that lay beneath his crisp white dress shirt.

He grabbed both of her wrists and held them in one of his large hands. "First," he said slowly, wrapping the tie around her wrists and securing them, "I am going to tie this so your hands are bound." He yanked the tie to tighten the knot he'd formed. Her wrists weren't going anywhere. "Then, I'm going to pick you up, bring you to the bed, and have my dirty way with you. Do you understand me, Mrs. Mason?"

She nodded, her body already panting with desire. He lifted her body easily over his shoulder again, carrying her to the bed. Her tied hands were placed above her head as he set her down on the plush white duvet, turning her over onto her stomach. He opened the bedside drawer and pulled out another tie that he'd requested be in there. Asher used it to tie her secured hands to the discreetly hidden clasps buried within the white tufts of the headboard.

She moaned, lifting her small, firm ass in the air as she writhed on the mattress, waiting. He stood beside the bed so she could watch him slowly unbutton his shirt, one hole at a time. He yanked the tails of his dress shirt from his pale pink pants and slowly shrugged it to the floor. Her eyes soaked in every ridge of muscle along his torso. He had an eight-pack he worked hard to maintain, and he was proud of it. It helped him keep up his stamina for his vigorous workouts in the White Room, too.

"I want to lick your stomach," she said honestly.

"You will," he said. "But a real gentleman always puts his woman first. Don't you agree?"

She chuckled. "A good southern boy certainly does," she murmured. "And I know you were raised right."

He grinned, unzipping his pants and stepping out of them. He slowly lowered his silk boxers, letting Vironica take in the whole of him. He knew he was long, and she was a small woman. Her eyes grew big and greedy, and she bucked against her restraints. "Don't make me wait, jockey. I love foreplay, but I came for the that," she said bluntly.

He laughed, holding himself in his hand and stroking his length. "What—this? You came to the races today to ride my stallion?" he teased.

She nearly panted as she looked at him with longing. "Yes," she breathed out. "It's been a long time since my last visit to the

White Room, and it wasn't as . . . fulfilling as I'd hoped. I have no doubt your fine stallion will sweep the entire race and wind up in the Winner's Circle," she said, biting her lower lip in desire.

"I guarantee you it will," Asher said, chuckling. He pulled another item from the bedside table and concealed it as he climbed onto the bed behind her, spreading her legs apart with his hands. He used the long white feather to slowly trace a path down her back and over the soft mounds of her behind. Her legs flexed with desire at the delicate tickling along the sensitive flesh of her backside.

Asher traced the tip of the feather along the slope of her inner thigh, leaning over and running his warm tongue over her pebbled flesh. He jockeyed between tongue and feather, teasing her, but not giving her the release she needed. He wanted her wet and ready when he pushed deep inside of her. He slowly tickled the feather over the outside of her soft, silky folds of skin between her legs, running it right up the center. She gasped, her body writhing under the restraints of the ties. She spread her legs and arched up, silently pleading with him to take her.

His mouth crashed down, hard and demanding, on her slick, wet lips. He used his hands to steady her hips as he buried his face into her from behind. She screamed as ripples of pleasure raced up her body, his tongue lashing out and plunging deep within her core. He took his time there, even knowing she was more than ready for his cock. He slowly, achingly slid two fingers partway in between her lips, rubbing her clit with his thumb. She lifted her backside in the air, trying to push her hips against him for his fingers to ride deeper.

He breathed warm against the soft flesh of her ass, asking quietly, "Is this what you want?" He pushed his fingers all the way in, arching them against her G-spot and moving them back and forth with precision before pulling them out slowly, letting her feel their absence.

"Yes!" she cried. "Oh God, yes! I want more of that . . . please."

He drove his fingers back inside her, using his other hand to cup and press her mons. She ground into him, squirming under his touch. Her moan was long and slow, more like a mewl, as her hips danced in a seductive circular motion and she came against his hand. He leaned over and licked straight up her wet opening.

"Mmm," he sighed. "You're more than ready for me, Wendy. Do you want me to take you like this, and ride you from behind? Or will you let me turn you over so I can look into your eyes while I fuck you?"

Her rhythm slowed and she turned her head, looking at Asher over her shoulder. "Turn me around. I want your lips on my nipples when you take me, jockey."

Asher slowly turned Vironica onto her back, her hands still secured above her head. He picked up the feather and ran it from her throat, down between her breasts, over her nipples, along the ridges of her slightly curved stomach, and back to her pussy. He ran the feathery tip over her clitoris, her body shaking from the aftershocks of her orgasm and the delicate, teasing sensation of the feather.

"Do you have any idea how beautiful you look when you come?" he asked. He set the feather aside, leaning down and trailing warm kisses over her abdomen and up her chest. Her pearls had settled between her small breasts, and he pushed them aside with his chin as he found her hard, eager nipple once again. He drew it in, gripping it with his teeth as he rolled his tongue over her soft skin.

He didn't know what drove him so insane about older women, but there was something so liberating and freeing about being with them. Asher lifted his body over hers, her eyes molten with lust as he met her gaze. "Whatever has you running in your real life, Wendy, promise me you'll face it—you'll stop hiding. You are far too perfect to dull your shine." He watched her eyes widen as he slid slowly inside of her, one inch at a time.

She spread her legs farther, wrapping them around his waist to pull him all the way in. He almost lost it when he was able to settle all the way inside her. It suddenly dawned on him how intimate and connected they truly were in this moment. So vulnerable to each other, so trusting. How had two people who were running, hiding from their real lives, come to find this safety in one another in the most unexpected of settings.

Yet they had. They were trusting each other to meet their most intimate, shared desires—without judgment.

Instead of moving fast and driving into her as he normally

would, he loosened the tie that connected her hands, surprising her. He pushed slowly inside of her as she worked her hands free.

Asher lowered his head and met her lips, drawing her plump bottom one into his mouth and sucking slowly. Her hips danced beneath his, allowing him to fill her but ride her at a slow and steady pace. Their pelvises met as he ground agonizingly slow, cupping her breast and massaging it in rhythm.

His mouth covered hers now and his tongue explored, meeting and matching her strokes with softness and desire. Asher grew even harder when she sucked on his tongue, her hands wrapping around the back of his neck and pulling his head closer, even as her heels dug into the backside of his waist.

He increased his tempo, her heels urging him on as he bounced against her torso, their abdomens now slick with sweat from their shared pleasure. He pulled back, holding himself up with his strong arms as he looked down at her. No words were spoken as he drove even deeper, touching the farthest reaches of her core.

This. This transcended the differences in their age. As he looked at Vironica, all he saw was a woman who needed. Who was reaching out and wasn't giving up. Despite all she'd been through with the loss of her husband, her heart was still open, and she was giving it to him in this moment. He buried his head in the crook of her neck and pumped harder, faster, ready to cross the finish line and give her—and himself—that final release and shared intimacy they needed.

When her body arched into his, and her teeth sank into the soft flesh of his shoulder, he drove harder one last time, feeling his body shudder. Her insides gripped him as he came, as if pulling every last ounce of his desire from him, demanding just a little bit more. Her own soft cries of release died against the skin she still had clenched in her teeth.

He'd taken women in every way possible in the White Room. It was at their pleasure and his. But he'd never made love to a woman in this room—until now. And the thought terrified him.

He pulled out and lay next to Vironica, his hand tracing the long red braid that lay against the stark white pillow. Her eyes were closed and a small smile played across her wide mouth. "Oh, man . . . you certainly do know how to please."

His heart constricted. Suddenly, it wasn't enough. He realized he didn't want to move across the country. He was fucking done listening to his father's "advice" about what was good for him, for his future. He'd been lost for a long time without ever realizing it, fulfilling his father's dreams instead of living his own.

Even coming to the White Room was his father's idea of what a man did. And, yeah, Asher enjoyed it and had discovered and matured his greatest pleasures there. It was in this room that he learned his boundaries, his deepest desires, his passion. He learned control and how to give and receive pleasures beyond his wildest dreams.

But now . . . looking down at Vironica, he knew he needed more.

He was tired of living without the love of a real family. Without the love of an amazing woman by his side.

One amazing woman.

He wasn't foolish enough to believe it was Vironica, but she'd sparked a rebellion inside that he wasn't ready to let go of now.

He kissed her closed eyelids. "Thank you," he murmured.

She looked up at him, her green eyes bright with the remnants of satisfied lust. "For what, my dear?" she asked, trailing her hand along the hard line of his jaw, her fingers finding their way into his messy hair.

"For helping *me* find Neverland," Asher said, laughing. "I was honored to be your jockey today at the races. But more than that, you helped me realize that even lost boys like me can be free."

Her hand paused, and her mouth pressed into a serious line as their eyes met. "Asher, I promise you this—you are no boy, no matter what your age. You may have heard an answer to your heart's unspoken question today, but trust me—I've known many men and many boys in my lifetime. Yours is the heart of a man." She smiled up at him, still stroking his hair. "If I were twenty years younger . . ."

"I know, Mrs. Mason," he said, leaning down and kissing her lips one last time.

The bell chimed and Vironica rose, sliding into her silky coral sundress, her wide-brimmed hat in her hand. She slid her sunglasses on and covered her eyes again. Asher's heart sank for the briefest moment.

She wasn't his to have—but she'd set a new bar for what he wanted.

She blew him a kiss and turned to walk out of the room. At the last moment, she turned and lifted her glasses, placing them on top of her head. "You definitely earned your crown of roses tonight. I've never met a jockey with as much heart and conviction as you. You're not done racing, you hear me? You still need to run for the roses."

With that, she fingered her pearl necklace, winked, and dropped her glasses back into place. "But if you ever get discouraged along the way, and need a reminder of the champion you are, you know where to find me."

Asher smiled. He knew she wasn't his forever—of that he was sure. But he had a feeling he had a lot more to learn about love, and the only way he'd find it was to look beyond these walls. Though they'd shaped him into the passionate man he was, they now felt confining.

He quickly dressed, tossing his dark navy sports jacket over his shoulder as he looked around what had once seemed as familiar as home to him. He grinned as he shut the door to the White Room, closing it behind him for the last time. He'd run his last race there, and it was one for the record books; but he was confident now that his real glory days were still ahead, and love was the only race worth running for.

CHAPTER 4
SIMON

Simon Ellison sat behind the executive-style desk he had brought in just for this occasion. It was the desk he really used at his campus office, and he wanted the smell of the woman he'd be fucking today to be all over it—something to remember her by. It was a traditional desk and the only thing in the room that wasn't white. The dark mahogany wood glistened almost black, not a scratch to be seen. The scratches that were unseen to most people were beneath the desk, where his legs nestled as he worked at his dream job as a tenured literature professor. Every woman he'd ever fucked after his college days had, at some point, carved their name under his desk as a token.

Even if they knew their affairs weren't permanent, each and every woman loved the power his position held. Enough so that they were willing to be one of many to etch their names into the dark wood with pride. It was a badge of honor for them. For him? Nothing more than fond memories. He liked being in control, but he wasn't completely heartless. He remembered each and every conquest, down to the last dimple, swollen lips, or the sound of a woman's cries during passion. He was one for details.

There was a hesitant knock at the wide double doors to the White Room. "Yes?" Simon said, pretending to be interested in the stack of papers that littered his desk. He didn't look up as the door cracked open; it was a power play, a way to show who was in charge.

"Professor Browning? I'm here for our three o'clock. Sorry I'm a few minutes late. May I come in?"

Simon cleared his throat, looking up for the first time. The woman looked to be in her mid-twenties and was clean-cut. Just how he liked them. Girl next door.

"I'm sorry. Your name is?" Simon asked, sounding bored. He knew his unaffected demeanor drove his female students insane. He was a challenge they all wanted to conquer. He only ever allowed a few of his real students that honor.

"Brooklyn," she said, walking forward. Her intoxicating brown eyes never left his. She was haughty, sure of herself. She pulled her straight blond hair to one side, over her shoulder. It fell past the bottom of her firm, perky breast.

"Brooklyn, you said? I'm sorry. Which class of mine are you in?"

"Poetry—101," she said, arching a brow.

"Lovely," Simon said, pushing the bridge of his glasses back up his nose. His tortoiseshell frames made his gray-blue eyes look darker, more dangerous. He sat back in his tall leather chair and ran his gaze up and down the woman's body. She'd purposefully dressed younger for their "meeting," as he'd requested. "Well, Brooklyn, how may I help you today?"

Simon ran a hand through his wavy brown hair, thick like Dr. McDreamy's. He was often compared to Patrick Dempsey, though the actor had a few years on him, and Simon wasn't graying as much yet. He waived his hand toward the guest chair he'd staged in front of his desk. "Take a seat."

"Thank you," she said, dropping her composition notebook onto his desk and shrugging off her tan leather backpack. As she did, her breasts pushed forward, straining the tight Ole Miss T-shirt she was wearing—his alma mater. *Damn.* The girls he'd gone to college with had never been that naturally sexy.

Her hair was long and thick, flowing as if kissed by the salt air she rode in on. She looked fresh off the pages of a surfer magazine with her glowing tan skin, white puka shell necklace, and Rainbow flip flops that were truly worn in. He hadn't given instructions for a specific outfit to be worn; he just asked for college student attire.

He'd been thinking along the lines of a short skirt and tight sweater, but this sexy beach vibe was getting him harder than knee-highs ever could. He adjusted himself through his pants, eager to get on with this meeting so he could pull her onto the desk and lick her five ways to Sunday.

"I don't have a lot of time, Brooklyn. I have a meeting with the dean in"—he looked at his watch—"thirty minutes. So tell me what I can do for you." He took off his reading glasses and set them in his desk drawer as he inspected the woman more closely.

Brooklyn's lips were full and sloped slightly down at the corners, giving her a naturally sexy pout. Her makeup was minimal and flesh colored, keeping her fresh and youthful as if she'd strolled right in from campus.

He ran a hand over the five o'clock shadow on his face as he watched Brooklyn play with the ends of her hair as if she were nervous. He grinned. Simon loved being in a position of power, both in the real world and in this fantasy suite.

"Well, I was wondering if you could further explain the balance in that poem that we read in class yesterday. The one by Frost?" She opened her notebook and flipped through the pages until she found what she was looking for. "Nature's first green is gold . . . " she read aloud, her pace slow, her tone deliberately husky.

"You mentioned this poem was a great example between the balance of—hang on." She pretended to look over her notes. "Here it is. Between 'paradisiacal good and the paradoxically more fruitful human good.'" She took a deep breath and shrugged her shoulders, looking up at Simon. "What does that mean?"

Simon stood up and walked around the desk, leaning against it as he faced Brooklyn in the chair. "May I?" he asked, nodding to her notebook. Her mouth slid into an easy smile as she held it out to him. Their fingers brushed as he took the book from her hands. Real sparks shot through his fingers, slamming him right in the gut.

His eyes swung up in shock, meeting Brooklyn's heated gaze. He swallowed hard and looked back down at the notebook. *Fuck!* That wasn't supposed to happen. He reread the poem, laughing because it was, indeed, one he used when he taught his intro-level poetry course. She was a smart woman beneath that simple, beachy exterior.

"Well, Brooklyn, the idea is primal, really. The poem captures both the precise perfection of a transitional moment, while also suggesting that the Eden-like ideal must eventually give way to earthly dying beauty," Simon said, reaching out to brush the sun-kissed tresses that had fallen over Brooklyn's eyes as she looked down at the pages of the notebook. Electricity shot up his arm again, and this time his cock tightened. He heard Brooklyn take in a little breath of air, shocked, too, by their instant and real chemistry.

"So, it's like a paradox," she breathed out, sitting up taller. She pointed at the poem. "Green is gold; leaf is flower; Eden is grief."

"Yes. But by the order and flow of the poem, we see that it's a very natural process by which the cycle of life is completed. The subsidence, the sinking, the going down is—by the poem's logic—a blessed increase if we are to follow the cycle of flower, leaf, bud, fruit, into a full life that includes loss, grief, and change. Does that make sense?" Simon asked, closing the notebook and setting it onto his desk.

Brooklyn looked up at him through thick brown lashes. "Professor Browning?" she asked, her chest rising and falling quickly.

"You can call me Grant," Simon said, using his White Room name.

"Grant," she said, testing the sound of it. "I love hearing you talk about poetry. It's my favorite subject. I know I shouldn't say this, you being my professor and all, but"—she leaned in and pressed her hands against his chest—"it turns me on when you read out loud in class. I've gone back to the dorm many days and touched myself to the memory of your voice, your smile."

She blushed, but Simon knew it was part of the "game."

He touched both sides of her face, daring her to meet his eyes. "Brooklyn," Simon whispered, "look at me."

She dragged her eyes up slowly, first over his chest, then to his hard, stubbled jawline. She took her time on his soft lips, and by the time she met his eyes, she was nearly pressed against him. "Yes?"

"I can show you poetry better than I can ever read it to you. Will you explore another poem with me? Do you trust me?"

She nodded, standing on her toes as she drew closer to Simon's mouth. "Teach me," she said just before he dropped his mouth to hers.

Consumption. That's the only word that came to mind as he took her. She tasted like strawberries and her hair smelled of sunshine. His mouth raked over hers, pulling in the delicate flesh of her lips. The moan that escaped her mouth brought his hands to her ass as he pulled her closer. She nearly climbed on top of him, trying to get as close as she could while Simon leaned back against his desk.

Brooklyn hiked a leg up and he grabbed onto it, grinding into her as their tongues explored, tasted, learned one another. Simon adjusted, pulling her all the way up onto his hips as he stood. She wrapped her legs around his waist, and her lips found the curve of his neck, her hands losing themselves in his hair. He carried her around to the front of his desk, setting Brooklyn on its top and kissing her hard, his hands still cupping her ass. She frantically pushed everything from the desk's surface as she inched toward him, pressing her warm center into his abdomen as he stood nestled between her legs.

Brooklyn raised her arms when Simon eased her Ole Miss T-shirt over her head. She shook her full mane of hair free as he threw the shirt onto the floor. He looked down at Brooklyn's bare chest and inhaled sharply. It wasn't as if breasts were new to him, but hers were exquisite. They were high and perky, but round and full. Small, dark nipples stared up at him, begging to be worshiped. He ran his hands slowly down her slender torso, watching as her skin pebbled from the light touch.

"Jesus," Simon said, "you're almost too perfect."

Brooklyn laughed, pulling his head in for another kiss. This time it was slow, torturous. She sucked his tongue, hard and deep, as her hand lowered and found his hard-on straining tight against his jeans. She ran her hand along the length of it as Simon groaned, pushing back from the kiss.

He bent his head and gently took one of her nipples between his teeth, sucking it slowly before pulling the entire areola into his mouth. He bit softly before shifting to the other side and doing the same. Brooklyn lifted her hips, encouraging Simon to remove her jeans. He yanked them down her long, tan legs, along with her miniscule thong. Her legs were nothing short of perfection. Simon ran his hands up muscled calves and over her full, strong thighs. She looked like she rode the waves daily with those.

He reached back to grab his chair, pulling it closer so he could sit down. He rolled forward, spreading her legs open with his hands. *Damn!* She was completely bare. Not a single hair stood in the way of his tongue. She put one foot on either side of him, borrowing the armrests. She was confident and didn't seem to mind being on display for him. He leaned forward, blowing on the opening between her legs.

"Grant," she breathed out, leaning all the way back on his desk now so she was lying down, "I want to feel your mouth on me."

Simon traced his fingers along her inner thigh, loving the shock of her body as it twitched with sensitivity. He rolled e.e. cummings lines from his tongue as easily as if they were his own. "'I like my body when it is with your body...'"

Brooklyn's legs trembled. He blew on her sex again, letting her feel the warmth of his breath as his fingers ran up and down both sides at an agonizingly slow pace. "'It is so quite a new thing. Muscles better and nerves more.'"

His finger roamed lazily over the slick surface of her opening. "'I like your body. I like what it does . . .'" He lowered his mouth and ran his tongue up and down her center, pulling in the smell of her sweetness with each breath. *Honeysuckle.*

"'I like kissing this and that of you . . . '" he said, pulling her outer lips into his mouth, sucking full-mouthed over her clit as he took in all of her. His tongue lashed out now, running in smooth circles around her sensitive nub. She was so wet against his mouth.

He pulled back, rising as he slowly inserted two fingers in his tongue's place until she gasped out loud, her hips bucking to meet his hand.

She raised her head to look at him while he recited the last of the poem. Her breasts rose and fell in rhythm to the spasms of her smooth, flat abdomen. She licked her lips and kept her eyes locked on his as she unabashedly rode his hand toward climax.

"'I like the thrill of under me, you so quite new,'" Simon

whispered into her mouth as he kissed her, arching his fingers to hit her G-spot until she exploded against his hand. Her body tremored as they deepened their kiss and she rode the final waves of her orgasm.

When she was done, she let her head fall back and laughter escaped her mouth, her cheeks pink from exhilaration. Brooklyn scootched her butt so she was sitting more center on his desk now, watching as Simon stood, backing away from her. He slid his wet fingers into his mouth, sucking the fruits of her orgasm from each digit. "I love the feel of you under me," he growled, reaching for the clasp of his own jeans.

"And I suspect I'll love the feel of you under me," she said, her eyes growing appreciatively in size as he freed himself.

"I want to smell you on my desk when you leave," Simon said bluntly. "So that when I'm grading papers, I'll get a whiff of your scent and be taken back to this moment."

Brooklyn cocked an eyebrow, as if considering. But she smiled, twisting her legs around so she kneeled on his desk. Simon stroked himself as he watched her part her legs, her center sinking low until it was flush with the smooth wooden tabletop, as if she were fucking it. She rolled her hips in a slow circle and slid her wet opening back and forth, her hands massaging her round, taut breasts as he watched her.

"That's enough," he growled, his cock already straining from tasting her. Now all he could think about was that perky little ass grinding circles on his lap as she rode him like she had his desk.

"Your turn to sit, Professor Browning," she instructed. He hoisted himself onto his desk, twisting to face her. She brought her mouth to his, licking around the outside before pulling in his lower lip. He groaned, his hand reaching out to grasp the back of her head. Their mouths danced, as if they'd done this a thousand times before, moving in perfect synchronicity.

She eased her leg over him, lowering herself down his thick shaft, gasping as he pushed himself in deeper, farther, until she was sitting all the way in his lap. She wrapped her arms around his neck, pressing her breasts to his chest. Simon's hands firmly gripped her hips, holding her down while grinding his pelvis upward, going deeper still. Brooklyn threw her head back, moaning as he helped to lift and lower her with each precisely timed thrust. She fit perfectly around his cock, her insides clenching tightly around him with every stroke. She may be young, but she certainly knew what she was doing.

He took her nipple in his mouth, biting it hard this time. She screamed his name in pleasure as the ripples of heat tore through her and sent her over the edge, causing her to orgasm for a second time. Hearing her cry out as she came was more than he could bear.

"May I?" he asked between gritted teeth, trying hard to hold on before spilling over.

"Oh God, yes," she moaned as he thrust one final time deep inside her, her insides warming with his long release.

They sat still for a few minutes, their slick frames molded

perfectly together. As their breathing slowed, they pulled apart. Brooklyn blushed, lowering her gaze as she rose off Simon and sauntered to the bathroom to freshen up.

Simon waited for her, crashing into his leather chair on spent legs. A lascivious grin spread across his face as he thought about the feel of Brooklyn's weight on his lap as she rode him. The supple curve of her bare ass as she strode confidently to the restroom. She was unlike any woman he had ever met. She had more poise than the youthful student she was portraying, and more intelligence, too. A perfect balance of fantasy and real life. He hated the fucking rules sometimes.

He glanced down his legs at the cubby hole under his desk. It had once seemed charming to ask a woman to etch her name under there. He positioned it as a badge of honor and way to remember their lovemaking; but for Simon, all it had been about was power—his sexual prowess. *The Professor's Club.* Not one of his conquests had ever been appalled by his request; instead, many hoped to be remembered the most, as the best lover he'd ever had.

Charlotte. Portia. Monique. Elexandra. Camden. Alice. Francesca. Bella. Erin. Mary Elizabeth. Brandi (with an i). Chloe. Lacy. Laura Rae. Pallava. Breñe. Anastaysia. Ingrid. Elise. Marisol. Peni. Brandy (with a y). Gabriella. Charlie. Lucy. Helena. Rosalia. Jean-Luc. Jasmine.

Simon knew them all by heart. Could remember each birthmark, each ticklish spot, each kink. Jasmine had been his last conquest, another woman he'd met in the White Room. He was certain Jasmine was her identity and not her real name. And Jean-Luc was his one and only dip into a curiosity he'd been intrigued by. Their night together in the White Room had been heated and passionate, in a primal way. But Simon's heart belonged to the women he seduced.

Glancing at the names, and remembering all of the beautiful diversity he'd encountered over his twenty-plus years as a professor, he couldn't help but wonder why Brooklyn was so different. Why he suddenly wasn't as interested in etching her name under his desk with all the others.

She opened the bathroom door and strolled over, stopping first for a bottle of wine. She kneeled down in front of him and gently washed her scent from his cock with a warm washcloth. She looked up at him through hooded eyes. "I'm sure you've had many students on their knees under your desk before, Professor Browning," she teased, running her confident fingers along his inner thigh and causing him to harden.

Simon nodded, taking himself in his hand as he stroked up and down. "There may have been a few."

"How many is a few?" she asked, taking a sip of the burgundy-colored wine straight from the bottle. Before Simon could answer, she bent over and took the tip of his penis in her mouth. She began to suck, letting some of the wine dribble down the length of him. She swallowed the liquid in her mouth and lapped the wine from around his shaft. She looked up at him again as she licked along his sac, running her finger beneath the delicate and sensitive flesh. "How many, Grant?"

"Why don't you look for yourself, Brooklyn?" he said, grabbing her hair in a ponytail and pulling her head away. She sat up straighter, rubbing her firm breasts around his manhood, her nipples tight and pebbling.

"Ooh, I like that," she murmured. She turned in his grasp so she could face the desk, his hands still gripping her hair and tugging gently, sending tingles over her scalp and down her spine. She arched her back and poked out her rear end. "Tug it again," she whispered.

He gave her hair a firmer tug this time, wrapping his other hand around her torso and massaging her breast. Her nipple was so fucking hard beneath his touch. He squeezed it, pinching it between two fingers as he rolled the delicate nub with precision.

Brooklyn groaned. She ran her hand along several of the names, as Simon grew harder by the moment. Was she angry? Did it turn her on? He didn't know. The suspense killed him. He'd never worried about what one of his women thought before.

"Tell me about Portia," Brooklyn moaned, rising to her feet. She leaned over the desk, her ass in the air toward Simon. "Touch me, and tell me about how you fucked her," she said. "Did you take her on this desk, too?"

It wasn't what Simon was expecting. He rolled his chair forward, running his hands over the smooth flesh of her ass. Her skin was so clear and beautiful. He noticed, for the first time, a tattoo across the small of her back. It was in cursive and was capped on each end by the crest of a wave.

I crave a love so deep the ocean would be jealous.

Simon ran his hand over the surprising words. He wouldn't have pegged Brooklyn for a hopeless romantic. Despite his many conquests, he was one too. He just never found what he was looking for.

Simon pulled her to a stand until they were nearly back to chest. Her firm bottom pressed against his hard-on, making it difficult to speak. Her hair was still wrapped around his hand, and he trailed the other down the side of her face, along her neckline, until he stopped and cupped her chin. He turned her face to make her look at him.

"Brooklyn," he whispered, "you don't really want to hear about the other women I've fucked. What do you really want? Let's drop the charade." Simon turned her so they faced each other, Brooklyn's bottom pushed against the desk.

She jutted her chin out defiantly, pushing her pelvis against his own. He grabbed onto her hips, grinding himself into her center. Man, she was making this hard. He knew they were never supposed to share real information, and he *never* had. Why, all of a sudden, was he curious if Brooklyn was her real name. Or how old she was. And whether or not she got those insanely sexy legs from surfing.

"I want you, Grant. We only have a little bit of time left. I want to feel you all over me. I want to quiver beneath your fingers again. I want to hear you recite more poetry to me. I——" She paused. "I'm curious about your past. How many students you've slept with. I'm not your real student, but I can't help but want to be special. To be more than just another conquest. Even if it is just for a couple of hours."

Just for a couple of hours. The words punched him in the gut, a visceral reminder that this wasn't real. That she wasn't his.

She ran her hands along his chest toward the hard V at the base of his stomach. Her fingers tickled his flesh as they made their way to his hips, digging in as she gripped them. She looked up then, her rich brown eyes searching his so deeply he felt as if he were staring straight into her soul. Then she broke him with one simple line. "I want more than I know we can have."

Brooklyn held her head high, her eye contact never wavering. "But if I can't have it," she said, "then I want to give all of myself to you now, in this room. Leave my heart on your desk so you carry a part of me with you every day."

She turned and opened his desk drawer, grabbing the pointed envelope opener. "Guess it's time to add my name."

"Brooklyn," he said, grabbing her wrist as she bent to scrawl her name beneath the desk with the others, "not there."

He pulled her up, angling her chin so she met his eyes again. "You *are* different. I wish this could be more."

He ran his hand through his wavy brown hair, then pointed to the front center of the desk. "Write your name there, across the top, so I see it every goddamn day. I will smell you on my desk. I will think of you every time I read a poem aloud. I'll remember the way you wrapped yourself around my heart in just a couple of hours the way no other woman has ever been able to do."

She closed her eyes and took a deep breath, as if collecting herself. When she opened them, she bent over and began to scratch the desk with the letter opener.

"Fuck!" he hissed under his breath when he saw that she'd etched *Eden* into the dark mahogany.

"Why did you write that?" he whispered. "Because of the poem?"

She shook her head. "Because it's my real name. And even if dawn goes down today—a very natural cycle of life, you said so yourself—well then . . . you'll always have this as a reminder of our paradisiacal pleasure."

"Fuck the rules!" Simon said angrily. He cradled the nape of her neck and growled, "I want you, Eden. I'm forty-eight years old, and I've never wanted any one more." His mouth found hers—searching, questioning, demanding. "Is my age a problem for you?"

"Not at all. Though I'm not as young as you think," she admitted. "Is that a problem for you?" She reached down and took the length of him in her hand, stroking him back to life. "Outside of the White Room, I'm not really the young co-ed you asked for."

"I don't give a fuck how old you are, Eden. I just want you."

"Good, because I'm really thirty-four. I'm an English professor at the University of Wilmington," she said and grinned. "I've never had a long-distance relationship before, but I'm willing to try."

"What about the White Room?" Simon asked, growling at the slow, torturous pace she was setting with her hand. "And, my name is Simon Ellison. Not Grant. Not Professor Browning. I'm a tenured professor, though, in real life. English lit," he said, grinning back with a cocky half-smile.

"This is my first and last time in the White Room," she answered truthfully. She leaned forward and ran a trail of kisses over the firm muscles in his chest, playfully biting a nipple. "I should ask you the same. Can you really give all of this up? All those names under your desk?"

Simon's hands found her hair again as he brought his mouth to hers, demanding all she had and more. "Consider them gone," he growled.

"Will you recite another poem for me before we go," she asked sweetly, dropping to her knees.

She took him in her mouth and teased the tip of his penis. Simon groaned, closing his eyes. "'Whatever happens with us,'" he recited as she dropped her mouth over him completely, drawing him deeper into her throat, "'your body will haunt mine.'"

Eden moaned against his shaft as she sucked him. She came up for air, locking eyes with his. "'Tender, delicate your lovemaking . . .'" she said.

Simon grabbed her under the arms and pulled her up as he sank back against his office chair. He pulled her onto his lap. "'The live, insatiate dance of your nipples in my mouth—'" He leaned over and drew her nipple in deep, sucking hard till she moaned his name.

"God, yes, Simon. More," she panted, sliding herself down his shaft again. This was becoming their thing, and he quite liked it.

She pushed her bottom down slowly, inch by inch, as he recited, "'Your strong tongue and slender fingers . . .'"

Adrienne Rich would surely approve, he thought as Eden took his mouth in hers, kissing him, her hands holding his scruffy jaw on both sides of his face. Her thick blond hair fell around them like a cocoon, protecting them in this moment.

"'I had been waiting years for you,'" Simon said, finishing a line of the poem and taking a plunge, deep into his future.

"Eden isn't grief," he whispered to her. "Eden is everything."

CHAPTER 5
EMMELINE

Emmeline paced the waiting room, unsettled. It had been weeks since her last encounter, and even longer since her only visit with Dom. What troubled her was that she'd never tried to remember anyone's name outside of the fantasy world that was created in the White Room. But Dom had stuck with her in a way no man had since she'd met her husband after college.

Emmeline was not her real name, of course, but it was close. Avaline Bellarose, wife of Henri Basile Bellarose, founder of the White Room. Because of his failing condition, he was no longer acting CEO. That had long since been passed on. With his time quickly fading, Avaline was spending less and less time in the White

Room, her itch no longer as important as spending her husband's last days with him.

He'd been encouraging her, though, to spend more time here in the actual White Room and not just overseeing day-to-day operations. But every time she stepped through those doors, her breath hitched when she remembered Dom sitting in one of the white leather chairs in his expensive suit, his tie loosened around his neck. She remembered the way he whispered her name as he slid that silk tie around her eyes, his fingers brushing the soft skin of her inner thighs. She couldn't shake him, but she was going to try.

Today she would lose herself in pure hedonistic pleasure. One with tenderness and seduction. One to completely take her mind off of a man she could never have.

When Avaline opened the wide double doors, she saw it was staged exactly as she'd requested. The lights were dimmed, and white candles danced around the space. White roses and her favorite moonflowers overflowed silver vases on nearly every surface, filling the room with a heady, sensual scent. The fire cast a warm glow over her naked body as she walked silently to the sound system. She picked up the glass of white wine she requested and took a long sip, searching for the music her body craved.

Camila's haunting "De Mí" quietly filled the space around them as she followed the sensual notes into the bedroom. Though she knew her time with someone else would never erase the feeling of

Dom from her skin, her lips, her thighs, she knew he wasn't hers to have, and the feeling gutted her. She was determined to leave him at the door today. This was the best way she knew how.

A woman her age lay naked on the expansive white bed in the sleeping quarters of the room. Her beautiful tan skin glistened against the soft white sheets and candlelight. The white silk cloth around her eyes and binding her hands and ankles to the bed contrasted with her skin in the most erotic way. Avaline loved all ethnicities, and the world was her playground. The woman on the bed today was everything Avaline was not.

While they both shared dark, nearly black hair, Avaline's skin was like porcelain, while her companion's was the warm color of a café au lait. The woman's facial features were feminine but angular, and there was power to her form, athleticism in a way Avaline's body just wasn't built. Avaline was all curves and sensual movements; the woman tied to the bed was sleek lines and athletic prowess. Even relaxed, the woman's body held ripples of muscles in her torso that Avaline couldn't wait to explore. She set thoughts of Dom aside, growing moist just looking at the beautiful woman before her.

She knew from her request that the woman was originally from Argentina. Her dark brown tresses fanned out around her on the white goose-down pillows, and Avaline itched to run her fingers through the tangle of long, thick hair.

In due time. Today was for languid pleasure.

She looked down at the woman spread out on the bed before her, so helpless, yet so powerful. Avaline knew she would acquiesce and do whatever was asked of her; but she had no desire for a sub. She wanted an equal, fiery partner. One who could match her stroke for stroke.

Avaline climbed onto the bed slowly, quietly. She lowered herself just inches from the woman's skin as she breathed her way up her body, starting at her toes. She made sure the woman felt her warm breath soft against her skin; her flesh already pebbling at the sensation. Avaline dipped, brushing her hard nipples across the woman's sensitive thighs, running them over her stomach and up her torso. She leaned forward, lightly brushing her lips over the woman's ear. "I've been watching you," Avaline said, gently biting the woman's lobe. Her body arched in response and brushed against Avaline's. Soft on soft. Even with muscular edges, women were just softer.

"¿Cuál es tu nombre, belleza ardiente?" Avaline asked, lowering herself onto the bed next to the woman and slowly trailing her hand down the flat valley between her cleavage. The woman had no body fat. She was like a sleek and powerful cheetah.

The woman turned her head, arching her small, firm breasts toward Avaline. "My name is Maricruz. I go by Cruz."

"Maricruz," Avaline echoed, her Castilian accent rolling the R with a sensuality the Spanish language was known for. "Fitting. My name is Emmeline, but you will not call me by my name. Our time together will be mostly silent, with only our bodies speaking. ¿Lo entiendes?"

Cruz nodded her head, sinking languidly onto the silken sheets. Each movement of her flawless tan skin sent waves of heat to Avaline's center. The woman's body was a masterpiece. Avaline ran her hand along Cruz's torso, loving the way the muscles constricted hard and firm beneath her touch. She brought her lips to the soft skin, running her tongue flat against the taught flesh and tracing a circle around her belly button. She slid her tongue up the woman's body, between her breasts, and to her throat. She drew the delicate skin along her clavicle into her mouth and began sucking. The quick intake of air told Avaline that Maricruz was responding to the warm sensation of mouth on skin.

Avaline lowered her hand and placed it on Cruz's thigh, squeezing it. It was muscular and powerful, even while relaxed. "Have you ever been with a woman before, Maricruz?" Avaline asked, her fingers finding their way to the thick tangle of curls between the woman's legs.

Cruz shook her head no, biting her lip as Avaline trailed her manicured nail up and down the outside of her center. "I will make you love the touch of a woman. There is nothing more *profundamente conectando* as feminine sensuality. I bet if you were unbound, you would be a wildcat in bed," Avaline said, chuckling softly. She brought her mouth down to Maricruz's, brushing her tongue lightly against the soft opening.

"Making love to a woman is freeing, Maricruz. I know a woman's body because I have one. I know where to touch you, where to taste you . . . how to fuck you," she said, sliding her finger into Cruz's tight opening. "Jesús, estás apretado," Avaline gasped, slowing her movements to a sensual rubbing back and forth.

She lowered her mouth to Maricruz's and kissed her harder this time, letting her finger sink all the way in as she did. Her finger languidly explored Cruz as she took time to savor the sweet taste of the woman's mouth. Cruz was already reaching out for more by raising her head to meet Avaline's kiss, pushing her torso up so their bodies brushed.

Avaline pulled back, watching Cruz's head fall back against the silk as she increased the speed of her finger. She brought her other hand down and slowly rolled it over the woman's clit, helping her get even wetter so she could add another finger. Avaline soon felt her finger slide more easily in and out as she moved her hand in time to the heated tempo of "Bésame" that played quietly over the room's speakers. Cruz lifted her hips to meet Avaline's hand, begging for her to go deeper. She may be tight, but she was soft, ready.

Avaline squeezed Maricruz's nipple while slowly inserting a second finger down below. Cruz expanded to fit her, her tight insides clenching around Avaline's fingers as they curled and plunged, increasing the speed to bring the woman to her first orgasm.

Cruz's body shook as Avaline worked her fingers along her G-spot, her body surrendering. Though her chest rose and fell with her increased heartbeat, Cruz bit her lip, staying quiet as Avaline had instructed. She rolled the length of her body like a wave, opening herself to Avaline.

That was another beauty of being with a woman—she could give Maricruz as many orgasms as her body could handle. She rolled on top of the woman, taking her head between her hands. This time, she took her mouth more forcefully, demanding passion in return. She'd eased the woman in with her first orgasm, now she would show Maricruz how sensual a woman's lovemaking could really be.

She pressed herself against Cruz, her round breasts flattening against the woman's firm, muscular chest. Avaline could feel Cruz's hard nipples against her own. Leaning down, she took one into her mouth, even as she ground her hips against Cruz's, bringing fireworks to their cores. She sucked hard on each breast, drawing the entire nipple into her mouth and biting gently, eliciting a soft, muffled moan from Cruz.

"Hold on," Avaline said as she gently rolled off Maricruz's eager body to grab a surprise from the bedside table. She leaned over Maricruz and whispered in her ear, "This is supposed to hurt a little, but the pain will be intensely intoxicating and shoot to all the right places. If it becomes painful, you may tell me. Otherwise, do not speak."

Cruz nodded, but said nothing. Avaline leaned down, opening the first nipple clamp and securing it onto the woman's sensitive bud. She heard a sharp intake of breath and watched as Cruz's body tightened, then squirmed on the soft sheets. Avaline leaned over, securing the second clamp and letting it close tightly like a clothespin over the sensitive flesh. The clamps were connected by a small silver chain, delicate and shiny against Cruz's soft brown skin. Avaline brought her lips to Cruz's, slowly sucking on her lower lip as she lifted the chain, tugging gently at the tension. When Cruz gasped, bucking her hips, Avaline closed her mouth over hers, plunging her tongue in deep. Their tongues rolled and curled together, a desperate moan pushing from Cruz's mouth as she whimpered in sweet pain.

Avaline lowered her mouth to trace Maricruz's areolas, gently tugging the nipple clamps as she did. She knew from experience that the sensation of cold metal pinching hard against her delicate flesh while a warm tongue soothed the pain was a heady conflict of senses. Avaline trailed her mouth down Cruz's taut body, her hands grazing each side as she did. Cruz lifted her bottom to meet Avaline as she settled comfortably between the woman's legs.

She used her fingers to part Maricruz open, exposing her soft pink inner flesh. She ran her tongue slowly over Cruz's clit first, drawing in the scent and taste of her partner. It was spicy like cinnamon, sweet like oranges. She flattened her tongue against the tight nub, warming her center as she prepared Cruz for more. She reached up and gently tugged on the chain, sending intense tingles of pleasure down Cruz's body and causing her to arch, lifting herself to meet Avaline's mouth. She slid her tongue down, her hands gently teasing Maricruz's soft curls. Her tongue ran up and down the outside of the woman's slick opening. She was more than ready.

Avaline plunged her face into the woman's hot center, thrusting her tongue in and out. She wrapped both arms under the woman's thighs as she pulled her down, covering Maricruz's clit and mons with her mouth as she sucked hard, teasing her beyond reason. She didn't let go, even as Cruz bucked beneath her, her thighs shaking against Avaline.

She pulled back just long enough to free the bonds around the woman's ankles. Cruz's body was glistening with a light sheen of sweat, her body rising and falling as she panted for more. Avaline would give it to her.

She centered herself between Cruz's legs and pushed them back toward the woman's shoulders until she had her sweet opening high in the air. Maricruz was as flexible as she was muscular, and her legs easily settled on both sides of her head as Avaline nestled her face deeper into the woman's opening, lapping at the slick juices like a hungry cat. She put one of her fingers into her mouth and wet it before tracing her tongue up and down her opening again, back and forth. She burrowed her nose against Cruz's clit while slowly inserting her wet finger into Cruz's backside. If Avaline thought her pussy was tight, it was nothing compared to this. She heard Cruz gasp as she slid her sole finger back and forth. She arched it, hitting a sensitive spot and feeling Maricruz push her bottom against her hand. Avaline smiled, pleased that Cruz's body was responding so eagerly. She wiggled her finger inside with one hand, while sucking hard upon Maricruz's clit until, finally, the woman exploded again, lowering her knees and shaking against the bed.

Avaline was just getting started on pleasing the beautiful Argentine's body. She rose, leaving her sweaty and panting against the white silk sheets. She loved watching the rise and fall of her chest as she squirmed against her hand restraints. Without saying a word, Avaline went to wash her hands and face. She wanted the woman to taste her, too, and she wanted to be fresh when she did.

Avaline gathered an ice cube from the wet bar and walked back to the bed. She tugged at the nipple clamps one last time before removing them. There were indentations where the clamps had been firmly attached. Avaline rubbed the ice cube around the woman's nipples, watching the skin pebble and the areola tighten in response. She leaned over and suckled on each one, drawing them back to shape.

"Did you like that?" Avaline whispered into her ear, tucking a long strand of dark hair behind it as she did. The woman's hair was soft. Another day she would love to brush it for her. Though she knew there could be no other day. She sighed, not for the first time damning the rules and wishing they were different. Cruz nodded, licking her lips as if she had the same idea as Avaline. She was thirsty too.

Avaline peppered the woman's face with kisses before finally finding her mouth and gently drawing in her lower lip between her teeth. She sucked the woman's lip into her mouth and released it. "I want you to suck my bottom lip exactly as I just did to yours." She allowed Maricruz to gently pull her lip in, tugging at it with confidence.

"When you suck the lips on my pussy, it will be the same way," Avaline said. She sat up, swinging her leg over Cruz's head. She positioned herself just above the woman's mouth, facing the tall, white, tufted headboard. She held onto the top of the frame, gripping tightly as she lowered herself, sliding her wet opening over Cruz's mouth. She felt the woman's deft tongue snake out, licking up her center.

She moaned. *Damn! Women's mouths are so fucking soft.* She let Cruz's mouth come to her, tugging and nipping at her outer lips, sending waves of pleasure over her body. Cruz soon found her rhythm and began to thrust her tongue in and out as Avaline slid her wet opening across Cruz's nose, letting it hit her clit in the process. She wanted more though. She wanted to be filled, and this was when she missed a man.

She slid her wet opening across Cruz's chest, leaving evidence of her pleasure along the woman's warm skin. "You did good for your first time," she said as she took Cruz's mouth in her own, drawing greedily.

Cruz kissed her back, hard. "Oh Dios mío," Cruz whispered, biting Avaline's lower lip.

"Ah, ah, ah," Avaline teased. "There is to be no talking. Do I need to punish you?" she teased. Cruz nodded while arching her chest. "I am going to remove the restraints, but you are not to touch without being instructed, do you understand?"

Cruz nodded but said nothing as she rubbed at her wrists where they were pink from being bound for so long.

"Stay where you are," she instructed. She kept the woman's blindfold on, though secretly she was dying to see the rich depths of her eyes. She had a feeling they'd be dark pools she'd lose herself in.

Avaline stood, walking back to the nightstand. She silently slid into her harness, a large lifelike attachment at its center. "Roll onto your stomach," Avaline instructed. The strap-on also had a small, vibrating bullet attached, sending light tremors through Avaline while she waited to pleasure Maricruz. She knew how hot the woman's body was, begging for a full release. Avaline would give it to her, sending them both over the edge.

Cruz rolled slowly onto her stomach, her arms stretched lazily over her head. Avaline kneeled over her, breathing warm air onto the woman's neck. She pulled Maricruz's long, tousled hair to one side, pressing her nipples against her back as she did. Her lips latched onto the soft skin of her throat again, causing Cruz to bury her face into the silk sheets and moan.

"You've been a little naughty, so I'm going to have to discipline you. You must remain quiet while I do."

Cruz nodded, rolling her head to the side and resting it on the bed. Avaline used her hands to hoist the woman's bottom into the air. She kneeled behind it on the bed, eager to fill the woman's tight pussy. First, she reached out and spanked Maricruz's butt cheek, hard. Her skin smarted, leaving a bright pink spot. She slowly rubbed her hand over the cheek, massaging away the pain as Dom had done for her. Pushing the memory aside, she slid three fingers into Cruz's tight opening as she gripped her hip. Maricruz pushed against Avaline's hand, her damp opening sliding easily around her fingers.

"So you like this?" Avaline asked.

Cruz nodded, arching her back and pressing more firmly against Avaline's hand.

"Do you think you can take even more?" Avaline asked low, heated.

When Cruz nodded, grinding her center against Avaline's busy hand, she smacked the woman's backside again, causing her skin to burn an even brighter pink. She leaned over and gently kissed the skin, bringing softness and pleasure to the sharp sting of pain.

Without warning, she grabbed both of Cruz's hips and slowly slid the long, attached shaft into her wet opening, taking the place of her fingers. "Oh my God," Cruz moaned out loud, not expecting to be filled this way.

Avaline spanked the woman's ass cheek again as she slid slowly in and out. "No speaking," she reminded Maricruz, who moaned into the sheets even as she bucked back to meet the long, thick length of the strap-on.

"There you go," Avaline said softly, gripping the woman's hips as she pushed and pulled in and out of her slick opening. She knew just how far to thrust in, knowing where to hit Cruz's G-spot for maximum pleasure. She leaned over and played with the woman's clit from behind, even as she pumped her hips at a steady pace. The vibrating base sent waves of pleasure through Avaline's body at the same time, and she knew it wouldn't be much longer before she exploded with heat. She felt Cruz's legs shake as the woman thrust her body back against the hard shaft a few more times before releasing, falling against the soft sheets, her body spent.

Avaline pulled out, sliding off the harness and letting it fall to the floor. She slid into bed next to Maricruz and turned the woman so their bodies were facing. They were both glistening with sweat, their bodies easily sliding and coming together. Avaline finally let her hands find Maricruz's hair, letting them get lost in the long, soft strands as they kissed.

The pace was slow, sensual, their bodies still humming from their shared pleasure. Avaline took Maricruz's hand and led it down her body as she rolled onto her back. "I need you to pleasure me with your fingers, so I can release," she whispered against Cruz's mouth.

Maricruz nodded, making her way down Avaline's body, using her hands as a guide since she still could not see. Avaline reached down and pulled the white silk blindfold from around the woman's eyes, pure lust shooting straight to her belly when Cruz's dark, exotic eyes met hers. Her lashes were long and thick, framing wide, almond-shaped eyes. A small birthmark graced the corner of her right eye all sexy as hell. There was no denying the heat mirrored back to Avaline.

Cruz never wavered her gaze as she kissed her way down Avaline's body. When she got to her legs, she sat up, kneeling on the bed. "I've never done this before," Cruz admitted quietly.

"Use your instinct," Avaline whispered. "It's just like kissing my mouth."

Cruz nodded, bending down and kissing Avaline between the legs slowly. She teased her tongue around her center before inserting a finger, sliding it gently back and forth a few times. Avaline squirmed on the bed, the sensation and heat rising as it filled her body. "More," she moaned.

Cruz inserted a second finger, driving them back and forth in the same rhythmic method Avaline had earlier. The woman was a quick learner. She arched them inside of Avaline, hitting her G-spot. Avaline purred in acknowledgement. "Press down on the top while you do that," Avaline instructed, showing her how with her own hand. "And I need one more," she gasped out.

With her left hand pressing just above Avaline's mons, Cruz slid a third finger inside, finding her pace and hitting her G-spot every time. Avaline rocked her body against the woman's hand, thrusting back and forth as she fucked her palm. Finally, as stars exploded behind her lids, Avaline came, her body shaking as she released against Maricruz's fingers.

The pace of dancing fingers slowed while Avaline rode out her orgasm. "Come here," Avaline growled. Cruz slowly crawled up the bed and sat next to Avaline, her legs crossed in front of her.

Avaline sat up, too, facing her lover. "Thank you for trusting me today," Avaline said, brushing a stray hair behind Cruz's ear.

Maricruz nodded, her dark eyes never leaving Avaline's. "I can never see you again, can I?" she whispered hoarsely.

"No, not with the way things currently stand. Besides," she said, blushing as she lowered her gaze, "I think you will be my last female lover."

Avaline was sure of it. Not because of Maricruz, but because she still couldn't get Dom out of her mind. Every touch she experienced, no matter how thrilling, made her miss the feel of Dom's rough hands. The way she felt possessed by and protected at the same time when she was in his arms. No matter how much she tried to forget him, nothing erased the memory of their time together.

With each passing day, she was losing Henri more and more. Her heart burned with anger and despair as she thought of the man she loved more than anything deteriorating before her eyes. He was one in a million, they said. She would have to agree. And under other circumstances, that might be a good thing. When it's your shitty luck having the rare and fatal Creutzfeldt-Jakob's disease, not so much. Every day she watched helplessly as her husband slipped further and further beyond her grasp. Soon, the man she once loved would be unrecognizable, his mind no longer his own.

"Hey, are you okay?" Maricruz asked tentatively, pulling Avaline back from her pain. "It wasn't anything I did, was it?"

Avaline held the woman's chin, lifting her face so their eyes met. She leaned forward and slowly kissed the woman's warm lips, their gaze never parting. "God no, Maricruz. You were exquisite. So much so I have no need for another female partner. I'm content to end my affairs with women having you as my last lover."

Maricruz blushed. "And I think you have opened a doorway for me. I never realized how much I would enjoy my time with a woman. I think my path in this journey has just begun," she said shyly.

"You will make someone an excellent partner, Maricruz. We have a wide range of clients at the White Room. I encourage you to explore your tastes and limits within the safe boundaries you have here. Once you become more confident, you will be a lover to be reckoned with," she said suggestively.

"You said 'we.' Do you own the White Room?"

Avaline took a deep breath. "In a matter of speaking. But you must not share this information with anyone, Maricruz. Perhaps over the year ahead things will change a little around here. If they do, I'll introduce myself properly," she said softly. She thought of her husband, as he'd been when they'd first met. Then she thought of Dom, with his naughty hands and wicked tongue. "But my heart belongs with someone else."

Maricruz smiled, her eyes beaming. "He's a lucky man, el meu àngel de pell clar."

"My Catalan is a little rusty," Avaline admitted with a half-grin.

"My fair-skinned angel," Maricruz whispered. "Thank you for being my first, and for giving me this gift to know how gentle and passionate a woman can be. I've always suspected as much, but I was afraid to give into my feelings. I will never be afraid again."

The bell chimed softly, reminding the women that their time together was over. The women rose, their arms encircling one another one last time.

"I will never forget you, Emmeline," Maricruz whispered. "Segueix el teu cor—follow your heart. You deserve as much happiness as you've shown me."

Avaline watched as Cruz sauntered from the room, her long arms swaying in rhythm with the muscled lines of her sleek backside. She would miss the soft touch of a woman, but her mind immediately circled back to Dom and the hard, sexy planes of his body. She remembered his deep voice when he'd whispered, "I'm used to getting my way."

Avaline was too.

Shivers raced over her body as she lowered herself into the same chair she'd first seen Dom sitting in. She propped her legs up onto the table in front of her and parted her legs. Avaline traced her hard nipples with one hand as she lowered her other, pleasuring herself one last time, using the image of Dom's nearly bald head and scruffy five o'clock shadow as her muse.

She knew he was one to break the rules. Dominick was his real name, after all. As she reached her peak, she called out his name, knowing that when the time was right, she would move heaven and earth to change the rules and see him once again.

CHAPTER 6
AUSTIN

Austin Wells was tired. Every muscle in his six-four frame ached from his daily squash workout with his brother, Alec. He was a merciless competitor, as were all of his brothers; but his rivalry with Alec was legendary. As firstborn sons, and twins, they were constantly one-upping each other. The truth was, Austin was tired of that too. Especially when his brother crossed a line and started dating his highschool sweetheart, Deena. Sure, he'd ended it long ago, and there was no chance in hell he'd rekindle that flame. Still . . . it smarted. Austin's only consolation was that he'd had her first.

Today he needed to escape. To be pampered. He'd been

pampered his whole life, but this was different. Lately, he was feeling off his game, and it wasn't just because of Alec. He was tired of the vapid women who found their way onto his arm. The endless string of galas and fundraisers. Most of all, he hated his job. Investment banking was exhausting. He closed his eyes as he stretched out across the large bed, waiting for his White Room partner to join him. He had no idea which one of his fantasies would be fulfilled today. All he knew was that he wanted it slow. Asked for something relaxing. He wouldn't be playing dom today, that's for sure. He was too beat down for that.

The lights went off and Austin sat up on his elbows, straining to see across the room. When the double doors opened, a solitary figure walked through, a dark outline framed against the bright light from the entryway. Austin couldn't make out the color of her hair, but it was pinned up in a bun on top of her head. Despite his exhaustion, he grew hard in anticipation. Her figure was generous and curvy, just how he liked it. He liked plowing into soft flesh that cushioned him and could never understand Alec's preference for women who were all bones and hard edges.

"I was told you needed to be taken care of today," the woman said languidly as she neared the bed. As his eyes adjusted to the dark, he noticed her hair was a light brown, copper highlights framing her face. It must be long, too, because it was a large bun that sat on top of her head, held together with two sharp sticks. "Roll over," she said, her tone seductive yet comforting.

Austin flipped over onto his stomach, his bare ass flexing when soft hands began gliding over it. He felt her weight as she climbed onto the bed, her soft silk robe teasing his skin as she lowered herself onto his upper thighs. He inhaled sharply when her hot opening pressed bare against the soft fuzz of his hairy legs. He smelled the lotion before he felt it, warm against his skin. Vanilla, and something exotic he couldn't place.

Her hands were soft but firm as they eased over his tired muscles in a sensual pattern, putting pressure exactly where he needed it until they softened, complied. Austin ached to turn over and look her in the eyes as he slid her down onto his rock hard cock. But she wasn't done, and he needed more.

The woman leaned over and massaged the knots from his neck, his shoulders. Muscles he'd forgotten about released stored tension as his body gave over to the relaxing strokes of her hands. He must have dozed off for a few minutes because when he cracked his eyes open, the woman's hands were pressing into the soles of his feet. He couldn't hold back his moan as her thumb ran along the inside of his foot, circling his big toe and cupping it, stroking it back and forth in her tight grasp as if it were something else.

He turned over onto his back and propped himself up to get a better look at the woman with the exceptionally skilled hands. She was tall, too, with broad shoulders and generous breasts. The silk robe she had on did little to hide how big they were, their large areolas visible through the white fabric as her dark brown nipples stood eagerly at attention. He sat up, inching his way to the end of the bed where she stood.

Austin slid a hand under the soft silk to find even softer skin. Her eyes never left his as he cupped the bottom of her large breast, loving the feel of it tumbling over the sides of his palm. He rolled his hand around the soft flesh, rubbing her puckered nipple until it grew hard. Austin pushed the silk fabric aside so he could take it in his mouth. Her quick intake of air told him she liked the soft suckling, the gentle roll of his tongue. He slid his other hand lower, moving the long, flowy silk of her robe aside to reveal full, thick legs. Soft. They were so soft. He ran his hand down the outside of her hip, over her round thigh. He grasped her flesh and squeezed, eager to be inside of her.

So much for taking it slow.

He took a deep breath, willing himself to slow the pace so he could fully enjoy his time with her. She was like a walking checklist of everything he physically wanted in a woman. He gently ran his fingers up her thighs, pleased with how they pressed together. He eased her legs apart with his hand, sliding the hard edge of his fingers along her soft opening. Austin tugged lightly at her nipple with his teeth as he slowly pushed two fingers inside of her, loving the warmth and tightness he found. She moaned, her hands in his hair as he tugged her nipple harder, his fingers slowly finding their rhythm below.

"What should I call you, beautiful?" Austin whispered as he lifted his mouth to her throat. His fingers danced between her folds, driving deeper as he stood. She took a sharp breath when he found her G-spot, her thighs shaking around his hand as he pressed back and forth, bringing her to the brink, then pulling back to delay release.

"What do you want to call me?" she asked coyly, pressing her body against Austin's.

She stood tall when his fingers slipped from her warm center. Austin licked them one by one as he watched her, their eyes never parting. Hers were the color of vibrant green jewels, and he wanted to get lost in them.

"Your name should be Jade," he said, his deep voice husky. "To match your eyes."

Though her cheeks flushed pink, she raised those sexy eyes to his and held them. "Then call me Jade," she whispered.

"Jade," he sighed, finding his way back to her center, plunging his fingers deep inside again. He slid them back and forth, slowly at first. His thumb teased her little love button, and Austin felt it swelling in response. Just how he liked it.

"And what should I call you?" she gasped as Austin increased his tempo.

He nearly lost his mind when her insides clenched around his fingers, growing hotter with each stroke he made. "Austin," he said, completely forgetting to use his White Room name.

"Austin," she sighed, "I'm supposed to be taking care of you."

"We have plenty of time for that," he said. He knew how to work his fingers, and knew he could make her come fast. He gently gave love nibbles to her large nipples as he added a third finger below. The friction of rubbing them back and forth not only hit the right spots inside, but covered her now-stimulated clit and caused little earthquakes in her core. Jade closed her eyes, rolling her hips to meet his hand.

"I'm not sure I can come this way, standing up," she said, her fingers lost in Austin's hair.

"Oh, you can," he promised, dropping to his knees. He flicked his tongue over her sensitive nub, sucking on the engorged clit. His fingers still pushed back and forth, driving straight up and massaging her G-spot.

"Oh God," she moaned, pressing against his tongue as her body began to shudder. Austin loved eating pussy more than anything, and was soon rewarded with her quick release. The whole thing took less than five minutes.

Austin grinned. *Take that, Deena.*

"Come," she said when her body had finished trembling around his fingers.

She headed toward the bathroom, and Austin didn't like the way he felt, as if she were somehow slipping away from him. She turned and nodded her head, inviting him to join her.

Inside the expansive, white, marbled bathroom was a large jetted tub big enough for two. Jade turned on the hot water and squeezed a clear liquid under the water's spray. While the tub filled, Austin watched as she lit a dozen white candles scattered around the bathroom. The room warmed in the glow of the candlelight, and he was getting his best look at Jade yet.

Her cheeks were round and pink; her eyes gently slanted up toward the outer corners. They were lined with thick brown liner, and her lashes seemed to go on for days. But it was her lips he couldn't look away from. Full, pouty, plump. They were every man's wildest fantasy, and he wanted nothing more than to feel them wrapped around him. When their gazes met, the twinkle in her eyes told him she knew exactly what he'd been imagining.

She turned away, unbelting the long, white robe and letting it slide gracefully down her body and pool at her feet. Austin's mouth went dry, her naked body now revealing the most beautiful, plump backside he'd ever seen. It looked like an upside-down heart, growing wider at the bottom. His cock tightened, bouncing against his stomach in the most primal way. He suddenly longed to grab her ass from behind and bury himself deep inside her—claiming her.

She walked up the steps to the tub and sank into the generous bubbles that now filled the water. She looked like a curvy Greek goddess and Austin's hand couldn't help but stroke himself to relieve the pressure as he watched her slowly sink into the bubbles. Her body glistened, slippery and inviting. She turned and looked over her shoulder, rubbing her hands over her curvy body. "The water's warm, Austin. Won't you join me?"

He wasted no time getting up the steps and sinking into the hot water beside her. He was wound so tight he almost exploded when she pressed her lush body against his, taking his face in her hands as her breasts pushed up against his hard chest.

She leaned forward and kissed him, parting his lips with a slow stroke of her tongue. It was something he rarely allowed in the White Room; but for some reason, he didn't hesitate with Jade. Her lips were too fucking soft to protest.

Jade's tongue pressed against his, rolling with it, sucking it in hard like it was something else. His cock responded and he heard her chuckle.

"Mmm, I thought you'd like that," she said, biting his lower lip. "I'm not done pampering you yet, Austin." She steered him to the outside ledge that surrounded the tub and eased him down. He leaned against the wall's cool marble tile, his head falling back in anticipated pleasure. The first flick of her tongue brought his head back up, their eyes meeting. Kneeling in front of him in the bubbly water, she ran her plump lips down the entire length of his shaft, taking him to his base.

He growled, pushing up into her hot, delicious mouth. "Fuck, Jade," he said, his hands searching for her hair. He pulled the long sticks out, one at a time, and released thick waves of hair as she continued sucking, twisting and rolling her tongue around the thick length of him. Her slippery hands wrapped around his shaft, played with his balls, massaged his thighs as she continued taking him deep inside her mouth. Austin lifted his hips, feeding his cock to her as deeply as she'd take him. He grabbed a fistful of her insanely long hair. It tapped against her plump bottom everytime she bobbed her head in front of him.

He'd honestly never had anyone be able to deep-throat him like that before. It opened something so base and primal in him he was almost mad with a desire to consume her. He lifted Jade up with her hair, his dom tendencies coming out to play.

"I thought I could just sit back and be pampered," he growled, turning her around and holding her with one hand cupping her breast, the other gripping the soft flesh of her hip. "But I can't. I like being the one in control. Is that something you're comfortable with?" He bit into her neck, pushing himself up against the soft rounds of her butt. She moaned, leaning back against him as his hand massaged her slick breast. He pinched the nipple while sucking the soft skin of her neck between his lips, aiming to leave a mark.

"What if I said no?" she asked, her tone raspy and breathless. Her body said yes, though, as she slid it up and down against him.

"You're not used to hearing 'no,' are you, Austin?"

He quickly bent her forward at the hip, positioning his cock at her center but not quite touching her. "No, I'm not. But say the word and I walk away. I like taking control, but my lovers are always willing. They beg for my cock. Have you ever begged before, Jade?"

He rubbed the tip of his penis against her wet opening, teasing her. She pushed her full bottom against him, inviting him in. "I'm not sliding inside of you until you beg me to," he growled.

Austin slid his hand down her wet back and fisted her hair again, lifting her up halfway. He rubbed her backside in worship before slowly dragging the ridge of his hand between her thighs. He wanted so badly to thrust inside of her, to feel himself bottom her out. But he was a master at waiting.

"I've never had to beg before, Austin. Most men willingly give me their cock," she said matter-of-factly.

"Oh yeah? And how many is 'most men?' Should I be concerned?"

She turned her head and met his eyes, her plump lips lifting into a half-smirk. "No more than I should be, right?"

"Touché," he said, slowly entering her and pistoning just the tip of his penis in and out, making her hot with desire, but not giving her what she really wanted.

"I can do this all day, beautiful," Austin said. He pulled out, rubbed his cock up and down her slick opening, over her ass.

"I want it, Austin," she said, panting. Her plump ass was pushed as close as she could get, his cock cushioned between her cheeks as she rubbed up and down.

"I want to hear it," he said, leaning over and squeezing her tits. He placed the tip of his head right at her opening and massaged it back and forth. "What do you want, gorgeous?"

"I want your cock, Austin! You know what I want, damn it," she moaned, pushing against him.

"That's my girl," he said, letting her slide her hot pussy down the length of his shaft. She moaned when she hit his base, her bottom pressed firmly against Austin's flat abs. He parted her cheeks so he could see her wrapped around his cock with her slick vaginal walls. She was so fucking tight.

His once-tired muscles were now relaxed from her expert massage, and his thighs flexed as he bent them, driving into her. Jade held onto the rim of the tub for stability, even as she pushed her hips back, inviting him in deeper.

Though she was curvy, her waist was narrow, giving her body an hourglass shape and something for Austin to hold onto. He took advantage of it, wrapping his hands around her torso as he found a steady rhythm, the bubbles making their bodies slick as he bounced against her relentlessly. She never missed a beat, throwing her head back and arching into him to meet him thrust for thrust. He nearly lost his mind watching that sexy-as-fuck hair bounce against her ass every time he pushed deep inside her.

He was so close to coming, but he wanted more. So much more. He pulled out and turned her over so she faced him.

She pouted. "Hey, I quite enjoyed that."

He leaned her back until she was sitting in the same spot he had been just moments before. "Then you'll like this even more," he growled. He sank to his knees and threw her legs over his shoulders. There was nothing he loved more than a hot, wet pussy. He leaned forward, savoring her scent as he took the first stroke with his tongue. *God, she is soaked.*

He pushed farther into her with his face, bathing her with his mouth, his tongue. Jade clutched the side of the tub as she lifted her hips to meet his mouth, pushing hard against his rapid ministrations. Her legs shook against his head, but he wouldn't let go. He wrapped his mouth around her clit and sucked harder. She couldn't move because her back was pressed against the wall, but her body writhed from the sheer agony of the pleasure. He was relentless, knowing she was so close. Her hips wiggled, the sensation riding the line between being too intense and wanting to explode all over his face. He knew that wiggle. He also knew to stay course.

His tongue flicked back and forth over her swollen clit until, finally, she exploded, letting him taste her even richer delights as she cried out in pleasure. Her fingers were knotted in his hair as she rode out the orgasm, his tongue still lapping at her sensitive nub.

"God, Austin," she said, her body quivering as the aftershocks raced through her. "Just—oh my God," she laughed shakily. "I don't even want to know where you learned how in the hell to do that." She pulled him up, taking his mouth in hers.

"But I'm so glad you did," she said, grinning.

He gave her a moment for her heart rate to settle, then offered a hand to help her up.

"Austin, our time's going to be over soon. I want to bring you pleasure before it does."

"Jade, you already have. But don't worry—I'm not leaving without finishing this." His deep blue eyes pierced hers as he lifted her up and carried her from the tub. They were dripping wet, but he didn't care. He carried her across the room to the large white bed and set her down gently, turning her over so her ass was in the air like a juicy, ripe invitation. He groaned. He'd been wanting to do this from the moment she dropped her robe.

"Have you ever been taken in the backside, Jade?"

She shook her head no against the soft pillows, whimpering just a little.

Austin was surprised, but undeterred. He slowly slid inside her wet pussy, getting himself nice and slick first. He wrapped his arms under her chest so he could cup her shoulders and drive even deeper. She moaned, her body arching against his in desire as he drove into her hard, one slow thrust at a time.

Her ass was too tempting, though, so plump and pliable. "I

want to fuck you in the ass, Jade," he growled, biting her ear. "Will you let me have that pleasure of yours for the first time?" She pressed her bottom against him in response, slowly rotating her hips in a seductive rhythm.

"I need to hear you say it, Jade."

"Yes, Austin. I'm all yours. If it pleases you, then I want you to take me that way. Just go easy, okay?"

Austin swallowed, hard. It would be difficult to go easy with such a beautiful woman offering him such a sacred gift—but he would try. He pulled her hips up, continuing to drive himself in and out of her sweet pussy to relax her. He licked his fingers, using them to wet the small, tight opening that stared at him from above his cock. It was so pink, so fresh.

Slowly, he slid from within her and placed his wet cock between her butt cheeks, rubbing himself against her to prepare her. He held one of her hips as he guided himself to her small opening. Pressing the tip of his cock against her, he slowly pushed forward.

Jade gasped when his head breeched her backside. When she clenched, Austin groaned, eager to push all the way inside to feel that extreme pressure wrapped firmly around his shaft. But he eased in slowly, leaning over to rub her clit as he did.

"There's no way to do this without a little pain, Jade. It's just like losing your virginity. Are you ready?" He kissed her back, running his hand up and down her soft skin.

"I'm ready," she whispered.

She screamed out loud as he entered her, slowly driving down until he was fully settled inside. "Oh. My. God," she moaned, her legs shaking.

"The worst is over. Now it's all pleasure," he said. He lifted his chest off her back and sat up tall, gripping her hips as he slowly rocked back and forth, finding a gentle rhythm. Every time he slid deeper, she pushed back, greedily taking in more of him.

He split her cheeks open so he could watch himself slide in and out; it was impossibly tight and sexier than hell—her letting him take her this way. He wasn't going to last long after all of their earlier play. He increased his rhythm, pumping into her with more vigor.

"Oh my God, Austin. Yes, fuck me!" She pushed back with equal exuberance, sending him spiraling toward the edge.

It was hearing her scream his name in pleasure that ripped through him. He couldn't remember the last time a woman had screamed his real name while he was fucking her. His body shook as he let out a loud bellow, releasing his hot seed inside of her ass. God it felt good not to have to pull out.

Jade was spent, her body shaking from the exertion of being taken that way.

"I'm sorry, Jade. Was it too much?" he asked. "You were so fucking sweet it was hard to hold back. My God, you are exquisite." He lay down on the bed next to her, stroking her long hair as her breathing evened.

"That was"—she paused, searching for the right word— "exhilarating. It made me feel deliciously dirty and wanton. I loved it, Austin." Her jewel-toned eyes were bright with passion as she looked up at him from beneath a wisp of her coppery brown hair. He reached out and slid the long strand behind her ear.

"I wish I could explore more of this play with you," she admitted. "Especially if it pleases you as much as it does me."

"Ah, Jade," he groaned, rolling onto his back, "it pleases me. More than you know. You would make an amazing submissive." He threw his arm over his eyes, his cock growing hard again just thinking about it. "If only there were time."

"I want to be taught by you, Austin," she whispered. "I know nothing about being a submissive, but I want to be yours."

He rolled over, growling as he took her hair in his hand and kissed her, hard. "You don't know what you're asking, Jade."

"I think I do, Austin," she said quietly, looking up from under long lashes. "And it's Becca. My real name is Becca."

"Becca," he breathed out. "I like that. You know it's forbidden, right? Seeing each other again. The White Room isn't a brothel. It's a fantasy. Once and done. Even if I wanted to, you're not mine to have."

"I understand the consequences, Austin. But I would break the rules for you," she said quietly. "I know that what you showed me is just the tip of your passion. I know you were going easy on me because I asked you to."

She sat up and straddled him. "Next time, I would ask you not to hold back. I would rather die from exhausted passion than live a life with mediocre sex."

Suddenly, Austin's body was no longer tired. He looked up at this beautiful woman above him—Becca—her hair falling down around her ripe body like Guinevere. He knew he would do whatever it took to possess her. Fully possess her. He knew from her temperament today that she would be strong, like the toughest steel; yet, when heated properly, she would be malleable and melt, bending to his every desire. And he had so much more to teach her. Being dominated in the White Room was hardly the same as a true dom/sub relationship. It was about so much more than just his cock. A partnership like that was about facing your vulnerability and breaking down the walls that caged you.

When you know what binds you, you know what sets you free.

He reached over, pulling a condom from the bedside table and rolling it on. He wasted no time lifting Becca up and sliding her back down onto his hard cock until she sat firmly on his stomach, taking him all the way in. She gasped with pure pleasure, dropping her head back and slowly rolling her torso and hips in a seductive rhythm that had Austin spellbound. He wasn't sure who was really in control at the moment as Becca cupped her large breasts and began trotting up and down on his cock, whipping him into a frenzy.

But he knew what he liked, and that was to be in control. He didn't need his high-powered job to find that kind of power. No, he would find it elsewhere. And it began with Becca.

He gripped her hips hard, stopping her. "My brother Asher is a lawyer," he said, no longer pumping inside of her. She pouted prettily, trying to roll her hips again to stir him. He gripped her hips harder, pinching the flesh. "I've never had a proper submissive outside of the White Room, Becca. You will be my first. But my family is well respected in this community. You will need to sign the confidentiality agreement my brother draws up. Then, I will show you everything you desire—and more. You are destined for far greater than mediocre sex, my love."

Desire clouded her vibrant green eyes as she realized Austin was willing to break the rules and suffer the consequences for her too. It was quickly replaced with white hot lust.

"You will be mine, Becca," Austin said, thrusting up inside of her as far as he could go. "And you will call me Sir."

CHAPTER 7
VIRONICA

Vironica Mason still considered herself an amateur when it came to the White Room. Her last visit had gone exceptionally well with the Wells boy. Asher. Yes, Asher had been more than delightful. She had no intention of ever dating again after the death of her husband Tommy, so the White Room was her escape. Her way to stay sane in an otherwise overscheduled, over-pampered life. Even women of class had itches they needed scratched.

Today she was fulfilling a longtime dream of hers, but she wasn't entirely confident she had the guts to see it through. Vironica had always been the sweet one. A southern-born lady of means. The wives in her social circle would full on seize if they saw her today. The last time she'd visited the White Room, she'd stuck to a comfortable theme: the Kentucky Derby. The wide-brimmed hat had hidden her identity for a while, until she realized the man she was about to fuck was a high-school friend of her daughter. That might shame some women, but not Vironica. If she couldn't have Tommy, she wanted 'em young. Someone completely unsuitable for her real life.

No attachments. Ever.

Vironica stood in the center of the living room, facing the double doors where her submissive would enter. She'd never before explored sex from the lens of dominating someone else. But, lately, she felt compelled to take control. After she lost Tommy, her world had shattered. Grief clung to her every day, often ending in Ambien and more wine than she cared to admit. But ever since the White Room, she'd begun to cut back on numbing out, choosing instead to live with eyes wide open.

Darling Asher had given her the confidence she needed to explore her sexuality again. That man had made her toes curl in ways she didn't even realize were possible. She'd loved Tommy with all of her heart, but because of his long battle with cancer, their toe-curling days were a long-forgotten memory.

Vironica adjusted her arm-length black leather gloves, gripping the metal handle of the riding crop she was holding. She was a born-and-bred equestrian, after all, and old habits died hard.

Her nearly four-inch black leather stiletto boots hugged her petite calves, making them sweat. But they were worth every fucking penny. If her ensemble didn't say "I will own you," then nothing would. Even if she were shaking inside, Vironica knew she looked every inch the classy, seductive dominatrix.

The door opened and a man walked in. Where Asher had been fair and preppy, this was a man's man. His broad chest and shoulders looked more like wings than flesh. There was not an ounce of fat lining his washboard abs. Vironica was soaked with arousal just from seeing the strapping man before her with nothing more on than jeans, a blindfold, and a thick collar. He took twenty steps in—exactly as she'd instructed—then sank to his knees on the plush, white carpet and waited, silent.

This was a thrill Vironica had never imagined herself indulging in, but seeing this man subservient to her was more than she could process. She would have to go slow or her inexperience would show.

She walked slowly across the white tiled floor, letting her silver metal heels do the talking. They clicked confidently, and Vironica stopped just shy of the incredibly sexy man in front of her. His black hair was short, the scruff along his jawline just enough. She reached down and grabbed him by the jaw.

"Your name," she commanded, trailing the riding crop over his chest.

"Callum," he said. The remnants of a Scottish accent sent shivers over her body, her flesh pebbling at the seductive rise and fall of his deep voice.

"You will call me Mistress while we are together. Do you understand, Callum? If you call me anything else, or do anything I do not command, I will punish you with my riding crop. Are we clear?"

A cocky grin spread over Callum's face. "What if I like to be punished, Mistress?"

She wasted no time raising the riding crop and stinging his stomach with a sharp *thwap* of the folded leather end. "Oh, you will be punished, Callum, because I know you've been a very naughty boy. Have you touched yourself without my permission?"

"I have, Mistress. Many times."

Vironica grabbed him by the collar and pulled him to a stand. "Take your jeans off, Callum. Let me make sure they sent someone worth my time."

"I'm sure I'll meet your needs, Mistress," he answered, unzipping his jeans at an excruciatingly slow pace. Her heart hammered against her tight leather bodice. Her breasts were pushed to perfection in the strapless black top, making her look larger than she actually was. It empowered her.

Callum slid his jeans down to the floor and stood, his hands waiting behind his back. Vironica gasped when she saw the size of the Scotsman before her, biting the inside of her lip in glee. He was certainly the most well-endowed man she'd ever been with.

"You'll do," she said. She fingered the long pearl necklace that rode between the center of her breasts and over the top of her black leather bodice.

She walked around Callum, inspecting him from every angle. She was dripping with anticipation and almost didn't know where to start. "Lie down, on your stomach," she commanded.

Callum dropped to his knees before he slowly lowered himself to the floor. Vironica stood over him, relishing the tight, hard ass that greeted her. She wanted to bite it, she discovered, and vowed to make time for that. She stepped her foot up onto the hard, round curve of his butt, jamming the sharp metal heel into his skin. "What is your weakness, Callum?"

He licked his lips, never once mentioning the sharp heel on his backside. "My weakness is confident women, Mistress."

Vironica smiled. That wasn't the answer she was expecting, but she would deliver. He needn't know the confidence was fought for every day after her husband's death. She used her foot to turn him over, once again admiring the long, thick shaft before her. Vironica wasn't sure she could accommodate the man's girth, but she'd be happy trying.

She walked until she stood directly over him, then commanded him to remove the eyes mask. Vironica remembered Asher doing the very same thing and chuckled to herself. Damn if he wasn't right. She wanted to look Callum in the eyes when she owned his body.

She wasn't prepared for the heat that oozed down her chest and pooled in her belly when their eyes met. His were a dark blue. Water she wanted to drink from. He was so impossibly sexy she couldn't get her bearings.

She placed her spiked heel on his inside thigh, pressing hard near his groin. His gaze never wavered from hers, but white heat seared his eyes. She pressed down harder, thrilled when his cock responded. "What's your greatest pleasure, Callum?"

"Isn't this about your pleasure, Mistress?" he challenged.

"And so it is," she murmured. "Touch yourself, Callum. I want to watch you stroke yourself."

Callum reached his large hand down, working his thick shaft. Vironica grew even wetter, needing to find her release.

"You look like you need something, Mistress. Tell me what *you* want."

Vironica swallowed, watching the slow sliding of skin on skin as Callum stroked himself. "What do you get from this, Callum?" she asked suddenly. She couldn't help herself. She understood what she was getting from the arrangement, but she didn't understand why someone like Callum was here.

"Besides an erection?" he teased.

"Why do you come here, though?" she pressed. "You hardly seem like you'd need to."

"Nor do you, Mistress. Yet here we are." Callum stopped what he was doing and stood in front of Vironica, lifting her chin.

Her whole body was shaking with raw desire, but she found her voice. "I never said you could stand."

"Then punish me," he growled.

"Is that why you're here? Do you like being tortured?"

Callum chuckled. "It's hardly torture to be fucked by such an exquisite woman," he said, lifting her pearls. He wrapped them around his fist and yanked her to him. "What can I say? I like a bossy woman who knows what she wants. That's why I'm here. It turns me on to see a woman who knows what she wants and isn't afraid to take it." Callum reached out with his other hand and trailed his fingers softly over the tops of her breasts. "Do you know what you want, Mistress? Why are *you* here?"

Her chest was pounding so loud she was afraid he could see her fear in her eyes. Or worse, her wanton pleasure.

"I'm here for connection. For passion. Something that's missing in my otherwise normal life."

"I think we all are," he admitted. "Otherwise, we wouldn't be here."

He leaned over, taking her mouth in his. His lips were hard, commanding. But his tongue was surprisingly gentle as it pressed forward, demanding its way into her mouth and battling her will with its heat. "Tell me what you want," he commanded between nips of her mouth, her jaw, her neck.

"I want to get filthy with you. I've never really talked dirty with a man before. It—" She stopped, unable to voice her needs. *Fuck!* If she couldn't even say this, how in the world was she ever going to control this man? That's what she really wanted, after all. To drop her airs, the persona she'd spent the last twenty-plus years building, and release the passion that was burning her alive most days since her time here with Asher.

"It what, Mistress?" He grabbed her chin, yanking it up. "Tell me what you want me to do to that tight, little, high-class body of yours."

His eyes were dark, stormy. She recognized a challenge when she heard it. She leaned over, her breath hot and close to his ear. "I want to get filthy dirty with you, Callum. But you will obey me in here. And so far, you've been very insubordinate. So I will start with your punishment, and then you will bury your face between my legs and eat my pussy until I come all over that sweet, thick tongue of yours. Are we clear?"

Vironica was trembling from passion and a new sense of confidence. She ran her long nails down his back, scratching him so hard she knew he'd have marks there tomorrow. The thought made her wet.

"Turn around," she commanded. As he did, she reached down, grabbing the first thing she needed. She clipped a leather-and-metal chain onto Callum's collar and yanked it, hard. "Walk to the bedroom, and do not look at me unless I say you may."

Callum squared his shoulders, muscles rippling along his back. But he walked forward, all while Vironica tugged against the chain, making sure he felt the tension. When they got to the room, Callum stopped at the foot of the bed. "Mistress?"

"Lay down on the bed, on your back," she said, unclipping the chain and letting it clatter to the white tiled floor. "I want your knees over the edge."

Callum did as he was told. Vironica lifted the string of pearls over her head, running them through her fingers, bead by bead. She walked over to where Callum lay and knelt down.

She trailed the beads over his large shaft, letting cool meet warmth. "You may watch as I do this, but you may not speak," she said. Callum lifted his head, watching as she circled the beads around the base of his cock until they were firmly in place. His cock bulged with the increased blood restriction. She stood, walking slowly back to the living room to get her riding crop, returning even slower to draw out his pain—and his pleasure.

She stood in front of Callum, her insides wet with power. Callum's jaw was hard, pulsing, as he looked down at the pearls circling him. She could see the raw passion in his eyes and knew that it turned him on, even while it was delightfully painful. Vironica lifted her riding crop and brought it down with a loud *thwap* against his inner thigh, close to the base of his cock. "That was for standing when I didn't say you could." *Thwap.* "That was for asking me questions that were not yours to know." *Thwap.* "And that was for kissing me without my permission."

"Yes, but you loved it, Mistress. I bet your panties are dripping with your desire for me. Bring your pussy up to my mouth. You wanted filthy. I'll show you filthy," he promised.

Vironica dropped the riding crop, removing one boot at a time. She slid her tight leather pants down her trim legs, revealing herself to Callum.

"Do you want to know the real reason I come here, Mistress," he asked. "The naked truth of what drives me?"

Vironica climbed onto the bed, sliding her wet center over his body as she straddled his chest, looking down at him. She nodded. "You may tell me," she said, reaching her hand back and cupping his balls as he spoke, rolling them in her small, soft hands. Their warmth soothed her, filled her with a desire to suck them, have him inside of her mouth.

"I'm just an average man. I work hard for a living and earn every penny I make the hard way—on the streets, risking my life every day." He gripped her outer thighs, squeezing so hard she knew his fingers would be a visual memory on her legs in the morning. "The adrenaline is something I can replicate in here. Fight or flight. Sometimes I'm the aggressor, and sometimes I like to be dominated by a sexy-as-fuck woman of wealth. I couldn't have you otherwise; but in here"—he yanked her in one swift movement until she hovered over his mouth—"I know you will come for me. And there's nothing sexier than that."

He drove his face into her hot, wet opening, her thighs shaking on each side of his head as he lashed his tongue out, dividing her center folds. His tongue was thick, hot, demanding as he ran it back and forth along her slit. "Ride my face," he growled.

Vironica slid her center over his mouth, pushing down against his nose and letting it rub her sensitive nub. She rolled her hips above him as he licked her, loving the hard grasp of his fingers and the soft lap of his tongue.

"I need your fingers inside of me, Callum," she said.

"If you're going to get filthy with me, Mistress, get filthy," he sneered, pulling his mouth back. "Do you want me to drive my thick fingers up inside your hot, tight pussy, until I slam them against your G-spot and make you come all over them? Is that what you want?"

"Yes," she breathed out. "Fuck me with your fingers, Callum."

He flipped her over like she weighed nothing. She was on her back looking up at him before she knew what had even happened. He spread her legs wide apart, eyeing her hot center. A lascivious smile spread across his face. "Natural," he murmured, looking at her strawberry blond curls. "Damn, that's hot."

He leaned over her, taking her mouth in his and owning it. "Sorry, I can't help myself. Guess you'll have to punish me again later," he teased as he drove two thick fingers all the way inside of her until she cried out his name.

Vironica clenched around him, her eyes rolling back as he massaged his way around her tight pussy with his fingers. Callum bent his head, his tongue commanding hers, in step with every stroke of his fingers below. Vironica screamed again when he bottomed her out, then bent his fingers and rubbed. "Oh, you like that, do you? I can feel your sweet juices flowing all over my fingers," he said, licking his way down Vironica's neck. "What shall I do now, Mistress?" he asked, his tongue finding her belly button and making love to it gently, torturously slow.

Vironica gasped at the sensitive place she never knew she had. Callum looked up and grinned. "Didn't know this was an erogenous zone, did you?" he asked. "What do you want, Mistress?"

"Lick me again. I want your head between my legs. I want you to taste me and have my scent all over your mouth, your chin, your lips."

A cocky smirk spread across Callum's face. He winked as he yanked Vironica to the edge of the bed so he could kneel on the floor in front of her. He dove between her legs again, licking up one side and down the other, lapping at her sweet center until she soared over the edge, her orgasm wracking her body.

Callum stood, his face slick with the evidence of Vironica's pleasure. "My God, you even taste expensive," he said.

Vironica laughed, sitting up. "Come here," she ordered. She gently unwound the pearls from his cock as he stood in front of her. "Turn around."

Callum did as he was told. Vironica cupped his hard ass in her small hands, massaging the round flesh of his cheeks. She leaned over and bit one side, hard, leaving teeth marks. His ass flexed from the pain, but he said nothing. She leaned over and bit the other cheek with equal force. She'd wanted to do that since the moment he'd walked in.

She stood up, wrapping her arms around him from behind so she could take his cock in her hands. He leaned his back against her, allowing her a place to rest her cheek. She pressed the side of her face against his strong muscles as she explored the length and girth of him with her fingers.

"Your fingers are so small and delicate," he said. "I love how soft they are against my skin."

"What else would feel good against your skin, Callum?"

"This is about what you want, Mistress."

"Oh, I want it. I just want to hear you beg for it first."

He turned around and faced her, looming over her now that she was no longer in her heeled boots. He lifted her breast free from her corseted top, kneading it with his large hand. "God you're fucking beautiful," he said. He leaned forward, taking her nipple in his mouth and gently teasing it with his teeth. "If this were my role play, I'd have these squeezed hard inside a set of clamps and strung up to a pole," he growled. "You would be the one begging."

Vironica's stomach tightened from the shock of the image he'd created for her, along with the lust she didn't know she had for such play.

Callum slowly unlaced her corset, letting it fall to the ground so that Vironica was completely exposed in front of him. It hadn't shaken her with Asher, but for reasons she couldn't name, she felt as if Callum could see deep inside of her, where all her dirty secrets slept.

"There's so much kink inside of you, Vironica, that needs to be freed. I can see it in your eyes, feel it in the way your body moves beneath mine." He peeled off her gloves one by one. "Suck me," he growled.

"Fuck my mouth," she countered. "I make the rules. You come to me."

Callum nodded, appreciating her command. He sat her on the edge of the bed and lifted one of his feet to the soft mattress. His thick hand wrapped tightly around his cock, stroking it as he lifted it to her mouth.

Vironica slowly licked her lips as she stared at the tip of his penis. She flicked her tongue out, catching a drop of him on her taste buds. He was sweetness mixed with a heady, earthy taste. She wasted no time taking him in, wrapping her tongue around his shaft and licking the veins that pulsed with heat for her. She tried to take him all the way in, but couldn't. He was just too long.

"I want you to fuck my throat," she breathed out. "Just like you want to fuck me."

"You couldn't handle it if I truly fucked your face, Mistress," Callum warned, thrusting forward and giving her only as much as she could handle. She loved the way he palmed the back of her head, thrusting his hips with the foot he'd placed on the bed for leverage. She cupped his sac, rubbing him as she rolled her tongue around his length—greedy. Wishing he wasn't right and she could take him in farther.

He yanked her off him, pulling her up gently by the waist. Turning her, he pressed his palm flat against her back so she was forced to bend over. "You like to be dominated, too, don't you, Mistress?" he breathed, rubbing her backside in slow, appreciative circles.

Vironica could hardly breathe, she was so off-kilter from his sudden aggression. But she liked it. It left her panting, wondering. He didn't wait for her to answer; he slid slowly inside of her, letting her expand to the width of him before pressing all the way back. She gasped, gripping the white duvet in her hands and biting her lip, afraid she would scream and not be able to stop.

"Let it out," he said, pulling back and slamming into her.

She gripped the blanket harder, pushing her backside toward him, inviting him in again and again. He let go of her hair and grabbed her hips, setting a pace so frantic Vironica had no choice but to scream out his name as he fucked her.

"Oh God, Callum. Yes!"

"What do you want, Mistress?" he asked between gritted teeth. "Do you want it fast? Or do you like it slow . . . deep?" He slowed his pace, giving her only a few long, hard thrusts.

"Both," she panted, her body slick with perspiration. She felt Callum run his fingers along her back, then heard as he placed them to his mouth, sucking her sweat off. "But I want it hard, fast. I want to feel you explode inside of me, Callum."

It was all he needed. He leaned over, grabbing her breasts as he pushed inside of her. He licked her neck, her shoulders, her back before rising up and taking her hair in his fist once more. And he gave her exactly what she wanted, at a pace that left Vironica dizzy, seeing stars behind closed lids.

She fell forward into the covers, biting the material as he pounded into her. "God, yes!" she called out, letting him ravage her. She was spent, exhausted, her legs shaking by the time he finally bellowed out, thrusting deep and hard one last time before his warmth spread out, filling her.

She took a few deep breaths, her body appreciatively tired. "You may go kneel where you were when you first came in," Vironica said, surprising herself. She turned around, tracing her fingers gently around the collar that still gripped his thick neck. The black leather against his tan skin sent shivers down her body, but she knew she was too tired for a round two with Callum. Her insides were throbbing and swollen.

She put her pearls back on and walked, otherwise naked, over to the shower. She could see Callum kneeling on the carpet in the entryway from where she stood beneath the warm, pulsing spray of the rainfall showerhead. Side jets massaged her tired muscles up and down her body as she sighed in gratitude.

Callum had both awakened and startled her deepest passions,

some she didn't even know she was harboring. She'd been playing dead for far too long after her husband passed. She'd been afraid to live fully, to take all that she really wanted . . . and needed, she now realized. Passion was more a part of Vironica than she'd realized.

She toweled off, wrapping herself in a thick, warm bathrobe with WR monogrammed on the breast. The room had certainly changed her over the past several months. And she was suddenly hot for more.

She sat across from Callum in a square, oversized chair. The white leather was cool against the back of her legs. "I get why you like to come here," she whispered. "It's to forget yourself. To be the man you really are inside, the one you have to hide from the rest of the world," she said.

Callum's head snapped up, his blue eyes piercing hers.

"Out there, you have to be hard twenty-four seven for your job, am I right?" she asked, searching his eyes. When he nodded, she pressed on. "In here, you can be as hard or as soft as you need to be. As you want to be," she acknowledged.

"Mistress—"

The bell chimed, signaling their time was over. Regret filled Callum's eyes, and Vironica wished she could give him the softness he seemed to need to balance out the unrelenting fire. But their time together was over.

She stood, waving her hand to indicate he could rise too. "Next time, Callum, promise me you'll let someone make love to you. Even if for just a little while. Let your guard down and just be Callum. Accept and give whatever passion you truly desire."

Callum tipped her chin, searching her eyes. He kissed her forehead, slowly running his hand down her wet hair. "This was exactly what I needed today, Mistress. *You* were exactly who I needed. But next time, I'll find a way to slow down, no games. You have my word. Now, will you give me yours?"

His eyes were sparkling, dangerous.

Vironica swallowed hard, butterflies swarming her stomach as he leaned forward and grabbed her ass, pulling her body toward his.

"There is so much heat in you that you haven't even discovered yet. Your body was made to be worshiped, to be fucked in every way possible. Find someone safe to explore that with. In or out of the White Room. Your desires deserve to be unleashed, your fears to be conquered," he said, letting her go. Without another word, Callum turned and walked out of the room with nothing on but the collar he'd come in wearing.

She appreciated the view on his way out, laughing when she saw twin bite marks already swelling with redness on both sides of his butt. Callum had lit something deep and primal within her today. She thought about what he'd said, her body tingling at all the ways she wanted to be taken, and all the ways she wanted to possess someone else in the White Room.

Vironica was grateful for the protection, for the rules in place.

Even though she'd let her walls down enough to both give and receive more adventurous pleasure today, she wasn't ready to let them down completely outside the safety of these walls just yet.

No attachments.

That was her reason for coming to the White Room. Vironica smiled as she walked out of the suite, leaving everything behind except her trusty riding crop.

She had a feeling she'd be needing that again soon.

CHAPTER 8
ARIANNA

A rianna Wells was not allowed in the White Room, according to her father and five overbearing brothers. Except she found out about it while snooping through her father's paperwork one afternoon. Arianna was the youngest of the Wells siblings, and as the only daughter of Anton and Miranda Wells, she was expected to toe the line and never appear as anything other than a proper daughter and one-sixth heir to the Wells fortune.

But her life was boring. She was finishing up the last year of her "Mrs. Degree" from State, studying marketing and business per her parents' wishes. The truth was she wanted nothing to do with getting married, helping with the family's other above-board business (Wells

Media—a publishing conglomerate), or toeing the line. What her parents didn't know was that Arianna was anything but the vanilla daughter they believed they'd cultivated.

Arianna had things pierced that her parents would never dream of on their proper young daughter. She was on her fifth tattoo, too—all of which were in places her parents would never see. The heart with infinity sign at the nape of her neck just below her hairline was the riskiest, but she always made sure to wear her hair down—just as Daddy liked it—when her parents were around.

From the moment Arianna discovered that her parents had helped cofound the White Room with their best friends, the Bellaroses, Arianna wanted in. Though her parents only owned forty percent, they were treated as equal partners; at least, that's what she learned from Avaline, her godmother and wife of Henri Bellarose. She'd gone behind her parents' back to confront Avaline, and it had paid off. Avaline not only let Arianna in on day-to-day business decisions—especially as Henri's health rapidly deteriorated—she also gave her a lifetime key to the White Room. One she used much more frequently than her brothers. And it was her delicious secret.

Her fantasies were usually pretty benign, all things considered. Arianna liked playing the nurse, the cheerleader, the naughty school girl. And she liked much older men. Her father would probably have a heart attack if he knew how many of his peers and business partners she had fucked over the last two years. The thrill of that made it all the more appealing. She loved watching her father's friends' eyes widen in surprise at holiday socials at the country club, or when they came into Wells Media, finding Arianna at the front desk interning.

The power she held in those situations is what drove Arianna. She loved power almost as much as she loved the thrill of the secret. The only condition was that she never let Avaline make her White Room matches for her. She requested that the other matchmakers place her with partners of their choosing, all under an anonymous pseudonym—Julianna. It was the mask she wore while in the White Room, one that gave her freedoms she wasn't allowed to experience in real life with the squeaky clean boyfriends approved by Anton and Miranda.

Today Arianna was playing the role of an edgy, punk-rock hair dresser. It was a weird request, but she'd had weirder. Besides, she loved dressing up for role-play. She smoothed her hands over her Daisy Duke shorts, admiring her choice of black fishnet stockings and Doc Martens. Covering her petite, but perfectly round, breasts was a white Madonna-inspired bratop, a white denim jean vest, and long gold chains that reached her bare midriff. Her belly button held four real diamonds all in a row through the piercing her parents knew nothing about. Arianna trailed her fingers over the fake henna arm tattoo she'd gotten specifically for today and wished it was one she could really bare.

The White Room arranged to have a white melamine desk in

the main living space to look like a receptionist's desk. A professional silver-and-white, leather salon chair was set up in the bathroom near the sink, shears and a razor awaiting. She'd tested the chair beforehand to make sure she didn't mess up while playing out this man's quirky fantasy.

For some reason, Arianna was nervous. She paced back and forth while waiting for the door to open. Then she sat down at the desk and fidgeted with the pad of paper before rolling the white gold-and-diamond Cartier fountain pen back and forth across the slick surface. The paper was heavy weight and engraved with WR in beautiful platinum scroll. Arianna was pleased with all the little touches every time she came to the White Room. It was the job she hoped to secure after graduating college in just a few months—director of customer experience. She wanted to lead the team of designers who created the fantasy suites for the White Room's clients. Avaline had already told her she would help convince her father it was a good career move; though, if it didn't involve a husband, Arianna doubted Anton would seriously consider her aspirations.

The door cracked slowly, a graying strawberry-blond head peeking its way through the opening. Arianna's breath hitched. She knew exactly who this man was. She just prayed he didn't recognize her. The man resembled a young Robert Redford, though she knew him to be at least fifty. Arianna squared her shoulders and met his steely gray eyes head on. Recognition flashed across his face when their eyes met, his lips tightening in a half-frown.

"What . . . ?"

The man hurried in, closing the door quickly and bridging the distance between them. "Arianna? What in the world are you doing here?" he asked, his face ruddy and flushed beneath his ginger beard that was flecked with a distinguished gray. "I—"

"Well, you came in for a haircut, did you not, Mr. James?" she said, placing the pen onto the pad of paper as she stood.

"A haircut?" He cleared his throat. "Yes, a haircut would be nice, Arianna—I just—"

"Baron," Arianna started. She cleared her throat. "I'm here for the same reason you are. And that's to give you a haircut. You may call me Julianna for the appointment, okay? And I promise nothing leaves this room. Ever."

Understanding eased the stress lines between his brows. He nodded and extended his hand. "Forgive my awkwardness and rude manners. I'm Baron. Baron James. And you are?"

"Julianna. I'll be your hairdresser today." Arianna circled the desk to stand closer to Mr. James. She ran her hand through his thick, reddish-blond hair, scraping her black matte nails along his scalp. "Your hair is beautiful. Thick. What would you have me do with it today? Just a wash? Perhaps a beard trim?" she purred.

"Actually, I'm going to have you shave it all off, Julianna. I'm getting ready for an Ironman, and I'd like to be completely bald for the race. Can you do that for me?"

Arianna swallowed. "I'm not sure I'm *really* qualified to cut your hair, Mr. James," she said, breaking character.

"Certainly you are. There's no messing up when it's all coming off," he teased, reaching down and fingering one of her necklaces. "Won't these get in the way when you're washing my hair?" He held the large golden cross between his fingers and grinned. "Nice choice. I approve," he said, chuckling.

Arianna blushed, looking down. She had to get over their acquaintance and brush this awkwardness away. She took a step closer, so they were toe to toe. "This isn't really going to be a problem, is it, Mr. James?" she asked huskily, looking up into his stormy gray irises.

He reached down and lifted Arianna up by the waist, setting her on top of the desk in front of him. "It's a little awkward, I'll admit. I never thought I'd come across someone I know in here. And certainly not a friend's daughter," he said, clearing his throat. "Does your father know you're here?"

Arianna leveled Baron with her deep brown eyes. "What happens in the White Room stays in the White Room, as you very well know. So it doesn't matter what my father does or doesn't know," she said, inching closer to his torso. She ran her fingers up his chest, trailing them over his shoulder and to the back of his head. Her hand found his hair again. "It's going to be a shame to lose all this thick, gorgeous hair. What will I hold onto when we fuck?" she asked, being purposefully suggestive.

"I simply came for a haircut," Baron said, his mouth twitching at the corner. "Why don't we start with that?" he asked, pushing back and putting some room between them.

She kept his gaze as she slowly removed one necklace at a time. "Sounds good to me, Baron. But just remember . . . you may be a pastor, but you're not *my* pastor. And just because you know my father doesn't mean you know me. Can we leave our expectations of each other at the door?"

Baron nodded, looking down at the floor. When he finally raised his eyes to meet hers, a white-hot heat filled Arianna's belly, overflowing and landing squarely between her legs.

"Consider them left, Julianna. Now, about that cut . . ."

"Follow me," she said, taking him by the hand and leading him to the bathroom. He stood in the center of the stark white room, tiled completely with marble. Arianna circled Baron slowly, running her hands lightly over his bearded jaw. "Are you sure you want to lose this?" she teased. "A lot of women like a man with a beard."

"Are you one of them?" he asked gruffly, his voice catching as she trailed her fingers down his buttoned-up shirt and to his flat stomach.

"I am," she breathed. "But I like a fresh shave too. All that bare, smooth skin." She pressed her body against Baron's, standing on her tiptoes to reach his beard. She brushed her cheek against his stubble, rubbing his coarse hairs along her own smooth skin. "You want it all off?" she teased.

"Completely bare," he growled, unbuttoning his shirt.

Arianna stopped him. "Here, let me," she said, taking over. She unfastened one button at a time until she got to the waist of his khakis. She tugged gently, freeing the rest of the fabric so she could undo the last two buttons. She slowly slid his starched blue shirt off his broad shoulders. He was thicker than a traditional runner, she noticed. But his torso was flat and narrow. She let his shirt fall to the floor as she pulled his white undershirt over his head, revealing a smooth chest beneath.

"At least I won't have to wax this," she said lightly as she felt the hard flesh. .

"I'm not into pain, Julianna," he warned. "I'm a pretty straitlaced guy, all things considered. Is that going to be a problem?" he asked, tipping up her jaw so their eyes met.

She swallowed, shaking her head slowly. "I like to push the boundaries just a little, but nothing rough. I like a little role-play, but at the end of the day, I'm honestly more about the substance than the show," she admitted. "But I'm happy to do this for you," she added. "I didn't mean it like that."

Baron chuckled. He held both sides of her face, lowering his mouth just inches from hers, making her squirm inside. "I know what you meant, Julianna," he said, their breaths mingling with their close proximity.

He was the first to back away, letting her face go as he walked over to the salon chair. "Should I sit here?" he asked, taking a seat before she could answer.

"That's perfect." Arianna wrapped a lush white towel around his neck and eased him back so his head was resting against the sink. The water was warm, matching the heat building between her legs. Just thinking about the scruff of his beard against her inner thighs made her wet already; it was a shame she had to shave it all off.

She ran her hands under the water, bringing it to his scalp. Her hands found their way into his hair as she worked the water through his thick waves. "I'm going to miss all this hair," she admitted. "I don't think I've ever seen you without it."

He grinned, his eyes closed as she massaged his scalp, her nails scraping suggestively. He moaned, letting his head fall heavy into her capable hands.

When his hair was wet through, she sat him up, running a towel in smooth, circular motions to take some of the moisture out. She loved the way his Adam's apple rose and fell as she dried his hair, just inches from his face.

"Are you as hard as I am wet?" she breathed out, picking up the sheers. Baron nodded, his eyes never leaving hers.

"I wish I could wash your hair the way you just did mine," he admitted.

"I'd love that," she said, suddenly feeling a little shy. The close proximity and intimacy of cutting his hair had her on edge—not where she wanted to be when she had scissors in her hand.

"I'm going to cut your hair first, so that it's easier to shave when I'm done—if that's all right. It's what my brothers used to do in highschool when they played sports."

Baron grabbed her other hand and tugged, nearly pulling Arianna into his lap. "I trust you, Julianna," he whispered.

Arianna knew he was talking about more than just his haircut, and her nipples hardened in response. She'd never looked at Baron through this lens before, but now that Pandora's box had been opened, she wanted nothing more than to jump in with both feet.

She brushed her chest against his as she leaned forward, taking a section of his hair in her fingers. She rubbed it absently before using the scissors to clip it off. Section by section she shortened his hair until it was nothing more than a brush cut. Hair fell all around the chair, but Baron never batted an eye at losing his beautiful locks. He kept his gaze soft and on Arianna the whole time.

Arianna ran a towel under warm water and squeezed out the excess before placing the heated cloth on top of Baron's head. She pressed down firmly, rubbing as she did.

"Mmm, that feels good." He sighed. "What's that for?"

"To open the pores. It makes the shave easier, and closer too," Arianna said. It was the one thing she did know after shaving her private parts for years. Arianna was adventurous down there and often took risks with racy trims and waxings.

Arianna picked up a bottle from the counter and straddled Baron's lap. Their gazes held as she removed the warm towel and poured Sir Hare Head Shaving Oil into her hands, rubbing it onto Baron's scalp. It was as intimate as she'd been with a stranger, sitting this close and doing something as personal as grooming him. The oil was slick and made her think about their bodies, sweaty from exertion and pressing against one another.

She took a deep breath before lifting the razor. Arianna ran the blade along his scalp from front to back, section by section. She pressed her hot center into his lap as she did. His fingers nearly bruised her hips he was holding her so tight. When she was mostly done, she reluctantly stood, finishing the back of his head until he was completely bare and smooth. She leaned him back in his seat again and splashed cold water over his clean scalp to close the pores, then rubbed his head dry again with a fluffy new towel.

"I'll put some lotion on after I'm done with your beard," she whispered into his ear, running her fingers over his facial hair one last time.

Baron caught her wrist and pulled her down to his mouth. He pressed his lips against her ear and whispered, "I'll be using that lotion on you, as well. And, yes, I'm just as hard as you are wet, if you couldn't tell," he said, bringing her hand to the large bulge straining his pants.

Arianna couldn't help but grin. She couldn't wrap her head around this man, this pastor, and the ginormous hard-on he had for her at the moment. But she couldn't wait to explore it further.

Instinctively, she massaged the bulge in his pants, but then stopped herself. "If I don't stop, I'll never finish this shave with steady hands." She closed her eyes and inhaled deeply, rising. She squirted the shaving cream into her hands and smoothed it over Baron's beard. She wanted to kiss those lips before the beard was gone, but didn't want to taste the shaving cream. She leaned forward, darting her tongue over his lips, taking in the musky scent of him, the clean, minty taste of his breath. She pushed her tongue between his lips, running it along his teeth.

When she pulled away, Baron cupped the back of her head and held her in place, opening his mouth fully and devouring her in a sensual kiss. Their lips meshed as their tongues learned their rhythm, pushing and pulling in tandem, sending goose bumps down Arianna's spine. When the fury of the kiss slowed, Arianna pulled back, laughing. She had shaving cream all over her face.

"Here, let me," he said, slowly wiping the foam from her cheeks and chin. "God, I can't wait to have you underneath me, Julianna. Make this shave quick. I can always touch it up at home."

Arianna nodded, her eyes held fast under Baron's seductive gaze, the corners of his eyes crinkling with amusement. For a pastor, he sure knew how to push her buttons. She couldn't wait to see just how straitlaced he really was, and how far she could push his boundaries—within reason, of course.

She squirted more of the white foam onto her palms and covered his beard fully this time, placing both hands on the sides of his face. Using her thumb, she removed the shaving cream from his lips. Arianna lifted the razor to his face, slowly pulling down as she'd watched her father do when she was a child. Nowadays, he walked the six blocks from Wells Media to have busty women in cigar-girl dresses at Beards by Bellarose do this very thing for him—though, perhaps, not *quite* like this, she snickered.

Arianna was glad Baron had come here instead of her father's posh barbershop. She liked being this close to him, warming with anticipation as the sharp razor slid across his tender skin. There was definitely trust here, as Baron lifted his chin and let her slide the sharp blade over his Adam's apple. There was nothing sexier than the sound of metal scraping against the stubble covering a man's hard jawline. When she was done, she washed his face with a cool cloth, slowly running her fingers across the smooth skin.

He looked like a different man now. Harder. Sexier. Raw. Not so pastor-like.

She swallowed hard, her mouth suddenly very dry.

Baron clasped her wrist after she set the razor onto the slick marble countertop. He lifted her hand to his face and ran it along his jawline. "Like what you see?" he asked.

"I like what I feel better," she whispered, straddling him.

He pulled her hips forward, sliding her bottom against his lap. "There is so much you're about to feel," he promised, his hands tangling into her shoulder-length blond hair. He lowered his head and brought his lips to hers, turning his mouth at the last moment so her lips brushed his newly shaved cheek. She lashed out her tongue, sliding it against the smooth, soft surface.

"That's a close shave," she said, her lips finding his. He kissed her hungrily, as if starving for her mouth. "Wait till you see just how close of a shave I have," she said, biting his lip.

He pushed up, making her feel the thickness of him against her core. Sliding her hips back and forth, she kissed her way along his now bare jawline. She'd never noticed how angular it was before. She leaned over, picking up a tube of aftershave balm. "First this," she said. "I don't want to leave you chafed."

"I wish I could say the same thing about you," he growled as she rubbed the warmed lotion over his bald head. Her insides grew hotter and wetter as she traced the circular shape of his scalp, knowing she'd be holding onto his ears when the time came. She leaned down and gently nibbled one before rubbing the balm into his cheeks and jaw.

"Enough!" he barked out as he gripped her hips and lifted her as he stood. She wrapped her long legs around his waist, kissing the soft crook of his neck as he carried her to the small kitchen area.

"Aren't we going to the bedroom?" she asked, looking around at the stainless-steel appliances and Carrera marble countertops.

"In a minute. I'm suddenly very hungry," he said, setting her onto the kitchen island.

He slid her jean vest off and ran a hand along the flat part of her exposed abdomen. He fingered the four diamonds that rested against her bare skin. "Nice," he said, brushing his fingers delicately around her belly button, sending goose bumps racing up Arianna's arms.

"Lean back," he instructed, yanking her hips so they were all the way at the counter's edge.

Arianna leaned against the stone countertop, her back arching and her nipples hardening at the cold sensation against her exposed midriff. Baron slowly slid his hands up her thighs, over the fishnet stockings. "Sexy," he breathed out, bending down and kissing her inner thigh as he let his fingers slide up under the frayed hem of her shorts. He massaged the inside of her thighs as he kissed his way down her legs. Slowly, he unlaced her Doc Martens, letting them fall to the ground.

The suspense was killing Arianna. She wanted to rip her shorts off and wrap her legs around his head, pressing his mouth against her hot center. But she wouldn't. The anticipation was driving her desire for Baron to the heights of the tallest roller coaster; she couldn't wait to free-fall, the addiction of adrenaline rushing to her belly as she climaxed from the thrill of the ride.

Baron's mouth tracing circles around her belly button snapped Adrianna back to reality as his hands dragged down her sides, sliding her jean shorts off with them. A wave of lust flooded her when he ripped the fishnets from her body with a precision that told her he might've done that before. After yanking the rest of the fabric from her legs, he picked one up and set it on his shoulder. He was holding her ankle when he turned his head and kissed the inside of her foot, at the most sensitive and ticklish spot.

Arianna giggled, then stopped when he slipped her big toe into his mouth, sucking it hard and sending waves of heat straight between her legs. She'd never had anyone suck her toes before, but she rather liked it. She inhaled sharply, holding her breath as he made love to her foot with his tongue. Her insides grew damp as she gave in to the sweet torment of his skilled mouth.

He kept her leg on his shoulder as he kissed his way down it. Arianna instinctively lifted her hips to him, but he palmed her stomach and pushed her bottom back down. "Not yet," he growled. "It was exquisite torture having your hands all over me in the barber chair. Now it's your turn."

"But that wasn't even that sexual," Arianna moaned.

"It was more sensual than you know, you little minx," he argued. "Stay put," he ordered. Baron went to the freezer and pulled something out, though Arianna couldn't see what. He came back over and slowly slid her black thong over her hips and down her trim legs. He drew in a quick breath, making Arianna smile.

"A heart?" he asked, staring at the closely trimmed hair pointing directly to her hot center.

"I told you I'd shaved for you too," she whispered, suddenly feeling a little shy and a tad immature with the heart-shaped design. She'd thought it was sexy, though, and it was something new for her. "Don't you like it?"

She hated the hesitation in her tone. Arianna was rarely gun-shy when it came to men, no matter what their age. But she suddenly cared about Baron's opinion of her. She started to sit up.

"I said stay put," he growled. He reached his hand out, running his fingers over her closely cropped hair, tracing the outline of the heart and letting his fingers drop to her center. "It's sexy as hell," he moaned, sliding two fingers deep inside of her.

Arianna gasped, loving the feel of his thick fingers as they pushed against the back of her, finding her sweet spot without hesitation. And this was why she loved older men. They knew what they were doing. Baron lifted her other leg, placing it on his other shoulder as he bent down, tracing his tongue along the outside of her wet folds.

"You're already so wet for me, Julianna," he moaned, pushing his tongue deep inside. This time, when Arianna lifted her hips to meet his mouth, he let her, placing his hands under her ass and pulling her tight against his face. He buried his head, sucking hard on her clitoris and not letting go.

Arianna screamed out, wiggling against him as he nearly drove her to climax just from the pressure he was applying to her sensitive nub. Before she could come, she felt something freezing cold enter her. She gasped, trying to look down and see what it was.

She felt the cold length slowly slide in and out, the sensation excruciatingly delicious. "What is that?" she gasped, pushing against the cold object.

He pulled it out, revealing a melting popsicle. He stuck it into his mouth, sucking her juices from the cold treat. She moaned, letting her head fall back. "Oh my god!" she said, laughing. "That's a first for me."

After finishing the popsicle, he dove back down, sucking the tasty drippings of the cold treat as they dribbled from her opening. He pushed his tongue deep inside again, licking her core clean from the sticky sweetness. It was too much for Arianna. As she came, Baron latched onto her clitoris, sucking it hard as he sent her soaring over the edge. Her legs were still shaking when he slid his fingers across her glistening opening and lifted them to his mouth, savoring the heady taste of Arianna's sweet juices riding the tropical notes of coconut and lime.

"God, you're sweet, Julianna," he said. "With or without the popsicle."

Baron lowered her legs, helping her sit up. He stared into her rich brown eyes, instructing her to lift her arms. He slowly slid her miniscule bratop over her head, freeing her firm breasts. They were no bigger than a small B, but they were sensitive, and Arianna loved her boobs. The nipple rings in each areola made them even more sensitive to the touch.

Baron inhaled sharply when he saw her bare chest, diamond sunbursts circling each nipple, held on fast by a thin, silver bar through the center. "Well, you're just full of surprises, aren't you?" he said, lifting his fingers and brushing the tips over her pebbled flesh. He bent his head and flicked each nipple with his tongue, biting the small nubs in the process. Arianna's head dropped back, her hands immediately shooting to his head. She held onto his ears as he continued sucking her sensitive nipples, nearly bringing her to a second climax as he gently tugged the jewelry that was piercing her flesh.

"I want you, Baron. I am literally dripping wet for you. I need to feel you inside of me. No more games. Take me to the bedroom and fuck me," she pleaded.

"I like it when you beg, Julianna," he said, yanking her from the countertop. She wrapped her legs around his waist once more as he carried her into the bedroom. He set her gently onto the crisp, white comforter, but she didn't stay put for long.

She sat up on her knees so she could help Baron undress. Arianna ran her hands along his hard, flat abs, envious of the ridges her fingers traveled. Her stomach was flat, but it wasn't full of muscles like his. They were rather sexy, and Arianna found herself wanting to lick them. She leaned down, indulging in her desire as she trailed her tongue over his skin, inhaling the fresh woodsy scent of his soap. She cupped his cock through his briefs, massaging it in her hands. After freeing Baron of the offending material separating them, Arianna took in the full of his form, pleased with what she had to play with.

As a triathlete, his body was near flawless. He had a scar running along one of his ribs that she wanted to know the story behind. She traced her finger over the bumpy skin, kissing it when she was done.

Arianna met Baron's eyes, sending a silent invitation to do whatever he pleased with her. She turned around and placed her head at the end of the bed so it was slightly hanging over the edge of the mattress. "Come here," she whispered, reaching out for his muscular thighs. He edged closer to the bed, standing directly above her. Her sweet, young body arched off of the mattress and she knew she made quite the picture. Baron moaned, rubbing his cock in his hand as he looked down at Arianna's lithe frame.

She grabbed his thighs and pulled him even closer until he was right above her, her head nearly between his legs. "Fuck my mouth," she demanded.

Baron closed his eyes, drawing in a sharp breath. "Are you sure?" he asked. "This won't hurt, will it?"

She looked at his impressive size, eager to wrap her lips around him. "We won't know unless we try," she said, licking her lips.

Baron squeezed his hard cock, lowering it to her mouth. She

took him in greedily, licking the tip first before running her tongue up and down the outside of his shaft. She looked up at Baron, who was hunched over, massaging her small tits.

"Don't be afraid to fuck my mouth, Baron. I want to taste every inch of you."

Baron groaned, thrusting deeper inside her throat. Arianna sucked harder as her hands twisted around his shaft, knowing the pressure would drive him insane. She used her hand to pump him, inviting it in and out of her mouth as he fucked her mouth upside down.

"Fuck," he grunted, holding onto the sides of her face as he thrust his hips back and forth, plunging between her warm, wet lips. He leaned over, sliding three of his fingers deep inside her, his thumb rubbing her clit as he did. His fingers dove in and out, matching the pace he was setting with his thrusting hips.

Arianna moaned, her insides clenching around his fingers as she came again. Baron stood up straight, trying to back away. She reached her hands between his legs, pulling his ass closer so he wouldn't leave her mouth. She wanted to taste him, more than anything.

Baron groaned. "I don't want to come this way, Julianna. I want to be inside of you. Feel your legs wrapped around me as I drive all the way into your sweet pussy. We don't have much time left. Let me have you," he said.

Arianna conceded, letting Baron pull back. "But you taste so good," she said, licking her lips.

"As did you, but I don't want to walk out of here without knowing all of you," he growled. "Kneel down, and let me take you from behind."

Arianna complied, kneeling on all fours and sticking her small rump in the air toward Baron. She could hear him slowly rub his wet cock as he appreciated his view of her from behind.

"God, you are so beautiful, Julianna. I don't know how I got so lucky."

Before she could answer, Baron gripped her hips and began to slide his long, thick shaft inside of her. Arianna wasn't that big, but she was eager to take in every inch of him that she could. Baron had, by far, the largest cock she'd ever fucked—with her mouth or otherwise.

"Let me know if this hurts," he said, then chuckled. "Though you seemed to handle it just fine with your mouth," he said, moaning at the memory of filling her throat.

He went slow, allowing her insides to adjust to his size. He could feel her vaginal walls stretch for him, inviting him all the way in. He gave one last thrust of his hips until his balls were pressed against her backside, her insides gripping him as he finally filled her full. She groaned, slowly circling her ass against his base. "Holy hell," she said, "you feel so good inside of me. Fuck me, Baron. I'm ready."

It was all the invitation he needed. He rocked back and forth, finding a steady rhythm as he bounced Arianna up and down his long shaft. She cried out when he bottomed her out, driving his hips in a slow, sensual circle. Her knees buckled and she slid them apart, lowering herself slightly. Baron reached around, covering her back as he cupped her breasts, squeezing them as he pumped slowly. She felt safe with his body enveloping her as it was.

Tiny tremors shot straight between her legs when Baron pinched her nipples—really hard. Arianna panted, loving the feel of his slick chest against her small back as her nipples burned with heat. He slowed his pace as he gripped her shoulders from underneath, cradling her body even tighter against his so he could thrust even farther inside her.

The pace was antagonizingly slow and sinfully deep with each pounding thrust.

Baron's lips found the delicate crook of Arianna's neck; he sucked the soft flesh between his lips as he increased his pace, slamming into her from behind.

"God, yes," she panted. "Come for me."

Baron lifted his torso from Arianna's back and raised her hips in the air, flattening her chest against the soft mattress. She was facedown, breathing heavily, when Baron gripped her hips again and resumed his fast and steady pace. Arianna loved the slap of his body against hers, the slick sounds of wet channels meeting hard lines. She clenched her insides tight around his cock until he groaned, growling loud like an animal as he plunged into her one last time, hard, pushing as far as he could go when he came.

Arianna collapsed on the mattress, lying all the way down as she caught her breath. Their bodies were wet and tangled, Baron's solid frame still covering hers. He kissed her neck softly, noticing her small tattoo for the first time. He traced it lightly with his tongue.

"So you're a believer in true love then?" he asked, kissing her head as he pulled out and rolled onto his side.

She turned to face him. "Of course I am. I just haven't met the right one yet, and I'm too young to get married anyway. What about you?"

"My wife died a long time ago. My children are grown now. Out of the house."

Arianna laughed. "Making them, what? About my age?"

Baron groaned. "Let's not talk about that so much, shall we?"

Arianna leaned in to kiss him, drawing in his full bottom lip. She ran her hand along his jaw, rubbing it back and forth. "Still smooth as a baby's butt. I think I did good," she said, beaming. "Though I would've loved to have felt your beard along my thighs, as well."

Baron grinned. "I wish there could be a next time. I'd grow it back out just for you."

Arianna's eyes crinkled as she smiled mischievously at Baron. "You never know . . ." she said, hinting she knew something he didn't.

Baron sat up, confusion drawing his brows together. "What do you mean? I thought the White Room was once and done? The rules—"

"Yes, but rules are made to change. Especially when clients' needs change. And I have it on good authority that the owner is looking to shake things up. You know the Bellaroses, don't you? I believe they go to your church."

Baron cleared this throat. "I do. Avaline was the one who discreetly recommended the White Room for me, given my profession. I'm still a man, after all. With needs." Baron grinned. "It wouldn't look so good for me to scratch that itch outside of a committed relationship, though. And I'm just not ready for that. I'm not sure I'll ever be after losing Sarah."

Arianna sat up and put her hand on his arm. "I'm so sorry, Baron."

They sat silent for a moment, each lost in thought.

"So, what changes are they planning to make then, if you're able to say?" he asked. "And how do you know about them, exactly? Don't you work for your father?"

Arianna grinned like a cat who'd just bagged the fattest mouse. "Avaline is my godmother. She's been letting me moonlight here to learn the business. I find it much more fascinating than publishing. Wouldn't you agree?" she asked, winking.

Baron laughed. "I certainly like seeing you here much more than at your father's office."

"Same," she agreed. Then Arianna's expression grew somber. "Well, you know Henri has been really sick for some time now. He has Creutzfeldt-Jakob's disease. His case was hereditary, I believe, which is rare."

"I knew he was having health problems, I just didn't realize it was so serious. They haven't been in church for the past six months or so. That explains why." He instinctively reached out to rub his beard, a faint grin lifting the corner of his mouth when his hand met the smooth surface of his jawline. "I'll reach out to them. Thanks for telling me. Do you know how much longer he has?"

"Days? Weeks? I'm not sure. He's already lost his vision and has no cognitive memory of Avaline or their life together. He transferred all of his shares of the business to her the moment he was diagnosed. Avaline has been running the business ever since, on top of caring for him. She really does love him, you know. Henri's family was always skeptical, but I know them both. What they have is real. I got the tattoo when I found out he was dying. A reminder that true love does exist. And that it never ends, even after death."

Baron reached over and cupped Arianna's chin. "You're awfully wise for someone your age," he said, searching her eyes. "So there's a chance I can see you again?"

Arianna shrugged. "You know my father would never permit it if he knew about our—encounter. He and Mother would never allow this to continue outside of the White Room, nor would your congregation look too favorably on you dating a much younger woman. Particularly one who's agnostic," she admitted.

Baron smiled softly, but nodded, understanding.

"I wish things were different," she said, squeezing his hand. "I've never felt as free and fulfilled as I have with you, Baron. I don't think you're quite as straitlaced as you think. I'd love a chance to loosen you up a bit, make you take a walk on the wild side," she said, raising her brows and grinning.

Baron laughed, rich and deep. "Well, if you find a way to change things and there can be a next time—even just in here—promise you'll contact me? I will honor and respect the White Room's rules and not speak of this outside of here. I wouldn't want to put you in a precarious position with your father."

"Nor would *you* want to be in a precarious position with my father." Arianna laughed. "But my lips are sealed. Avaline has been seeing a trend in clients requesting repeat visits with other clients they have already interacted with. It has never been allowed, but more and more people are wanting to revisit their favorite lovers, their favorite fetishes together. Once and done is fun, but the more you know someone, the deeper you can push each other. The more boundaries you release," she said, biting her lip.

Baron grabbed the back of her head, pressing his lips hard against hers, demanding more as he kissed her deeply one last time. "When the rules change, call me. My boundaries are yours for the taking."

Arianna watched as Baron grabbed his clothes and strolled from the White Room just as the bell chimed. Arianna fell back against the fluffy, feather-filled duvet and smiled, clutching the fabric to her chest. Baron was indeed the first man she'd call when the rules changed. She knew Avaline would need time to grieve, but she also suspected there was a personal reason why Avaline wanted to change the rules.

Arianna was determined to make sure they did.

CHAPTER 9
ALEC

Alec was pissed. Austin had trounced him at squash again for the third time this week. Something was wrong. Alec was never off his stride and usually wiped his twin's ass up and down the court. *Fuck!* He glanced in the mirror, taking in his long, muscular frame. Dark hair slicked back. He tugged at the hem of his French cuffs, the black diamonds staring back at him as if mocking his existence. A reminder of being rejected. And Alec was never rejected.

Until recently. For the first time.

And it smarted.

Alec removed the diamond cuff links and carelessly tossed them into the trash can in the bathroom before loosening his bowtie. *Fuck you, Deena.* He lifted the Jack and Coke to his reflection, as if saying *Cheers!* before letting the dark liquid soothe his bruised ego. He sauntered into the living room and glanced around, pacing restlessly. He knew what fantasy would be played out today, and it couldn't come soon enough. He needed to let out this pent-up energy. And there was a lot of it, thanks to Deena.

A quiet chime rang and a soft voice called out to Alec. "Sir, your dessert tonight will be served in the formal dining room. You may enter now. A gorgeous spread is all set up for you."

Alec grinned. *I'm sure it is.*

He crossed the room and slid open the nearly ten-foot tall frosted-glass-and-wood pocket doors that led to the dining area. He knew exactly where it was because his father practically owned the place. Each of the Wells sons was gifted lifetime access to the White Room upon graduation, but Alec had also recently joined the team, taking over legal operations with his brother, Asher. His sister's godmother, Avaline, wanted to take the business in a new direction and needed fresh blood in all key positions to really make that happen. He wasn't thrilled with his baby sister getting involved in anything having to do with the White Room. But Arianna really seemed to love her new role as director of customer experience.

Alec wished Deena could see him now. *Like a freaking boss,* he thought, scowling. But he wasn't going to let her get under his skin today. Not when he knew what was in store for him. He took a deep breath and shoved all thoughts of his traitorous ex aside. He was ready for whoever was waiting for him on the other side of the dining room doors.

Or so he thought.

Nothing could've prepared him for the gorgeous woman lying on the long table in front of him. Her skin shimmered under the light, warm and brown, a stark contrast against the sterile white of the table. She had strawberries nestled between her legs, covering her sweet center. White rose petals trailed down the length of the table alongside her lithe frame. Even though she was completely naked, Alec couldn't take his eyes off her long, muscular legs. As a once-semipro soccer player, legs were his thing. And feet.

Dear God, her feet.

Her toenails were painted silver and white. He walked closer to the table, clenching his fists at his sides. Arianna's customer experience team had outdone themselves, and he truly wanted to take a moment to savor the scene created for him, but his fucking erection was making that damn near impossible.

He cocked his head, trailing a single finger up the woman's arm. White chocolate lined her stomach, making a pathway to her generous breasts. More sliced strawberries filled her cleavage, circled each tight brown nipple, and lined her long, sensuous neck. Even her scrumptious lips were painted with melted white chocolate.

A white silk blindfold covered her eyes and caressed her flawless brown skin—dark and rich like a bold espresso. Her hair was left natural, a sensual halo of brown curls. He couldn't wait to get his hands in there while pressing her mouth to his cock later. Because, God, those lips though.

But first . . . dessert.

On a tall, thin side table sat a pitcher of cream and a fountain of white chocolate. As an athlete, Alec didn't usually indulge in sweets. But as a lover, it was one of his favorite pastimes. He leaned down, his lips close to the woman's ear, and whispered softly to her. "You look good enough to eat, sweetheart."

He saw the slightest twitch at the corner of her mouth, her lips pressing together in an inviting pucker. "Then what's stopping you?" she challenged.

Alec ran his hand gently down the length of her body, watching as goose bumps rose to the surface of her skin. He trailed his fingers between her legs and lifted a strawberry to his mouth. It smelled of sweet summer days mixed with the heady, delicious scent of this woman. Alec popped the fruit into his mouth, letting the juicy berry fill his senses. He grabbed another one and held it just above the woman's mouth.

"What should I call you while we dine today, gorgeous?" Alec asked in a husky tone.

"You can call me Lexie," she said. "And what should I call you?"

Alec traced her mouth with the tip of a strawberry. "Suck it," he said, watching as her tongue slid out, her full lips wrapping around the fruit to take a bite. Juices ran over her chin as she removed the strawberry from its stem with her teeth. Alec's cock took notice.

"You will call me Sir during our time together," Alec commanded, leaning forward and taking her tight brown nipple in his mouth. Her body tried to arch to meet his lips, but he palmed her abdomen and held her down so the fruit wouldn't fall.

"Usually I'm in charge in the bedroom," Lexie challenged.

Alec lifted his head and removed her silk blindfold, pinning her with his light golden-brown eyes. He knew they were panty wetters for the unusual shade that they were. But it was Lexie's stormy blue eyes that shot a primal lightning rod of lust straight to his stomach— and other places. If he'd had panties on, they would've been soaked.

"Well, we're not in the bedroom, are we, Lexie?" Alec said, recovering. He had to have the upper hand, no matter how mesmerizing her eyes were.

Lexie's gaze followed him as he walked to the side table, spooning some white chocolate from the fountain into a tiny pitcher that fit in the palm of his hand. It was exactly as he'd requested, as it always was in the White Room.

"Do you like sweets, Lexie?" Alec asked, his eyes raking her muscular form. "From the looks of it, you don't indulge too often."

"I'd rather be the sweet than eat them. But I'm willing to

reconsider . . ." she said, trailing off as he lifted the small pitcher and poured the white chocolate onto her nipple. He watched as her body spasmed from the intoxicating shock of the heated chocolate covering her sensitive skin. It was just like the low-temperature candle wax Alec sometimes used in the bedroom—not hot enough to burn, but warm enough to heat all the right senses.

Alec took her nipple in his mouth once again, biting as his tongue swirled her tight bud and removed all the sticky sweetness from her skin. He picked up a berry from between her breasts and bit into it, letting the juice run down his chin and over her skin to cool the triggered nerve endings.

His cock tightened as desire darkened Lexie's stormy eyes. There was nothing more intoxicating than a woman adventuring beyond her comfort zone. That's where the magic happened. Anyone can fuck. But it required passion, patience, and trust to release your fears and find pleasure with a stranger.

He leaned over and brushed his lips across Lexie's, licking the chocolate from her mouth.

"Mmm," she murmured. "I could get used to the taste of sweets on you."

"Ditto," Alec growled, reaching down and squeezing her nipple between the pads of his fingers. He tugged gently, knowing it would send sparks of electricity straight between her legs. "Don't worry. You'll have your chance. But we haven't even gotten started yet."

Alec shoved everything from the table that had been arranged perfectly around Lexie's body, yanking her to the end of the table by her feet. He placed those long legs over his shoulders and bent down, inhaling the earthy floral scent between her legs. He placed one of the plump, oversized berries in his mouth, the soft, round side facing out. Lowering his head, he ran the cold berry along the delicate folds of warm flesh between her legs. Lexie's hands shot to his hair when he gently pushed the strawberry into her wet opening. "I like my strawberries with a little cream," Alec said.

"Lucy," Alec called out, knowing the other woman would be right on time. On cue, a buxom blonde with an adorable pixie cut stepped into the dining room wearing a very revealing maid's uniform, her bare breasts fully exposed through the white and black bra that encircled and enhanced each glorious mound. The white ruffled choker was a nice touch, Alec noted. Though he would've enjoyed fucking the blonde, too, she wasn't on the menu today.

Lexie startled when the woman joined them while she lay exposed, fruit and flowers barely covering her naked body. Alec was unphased. "Please bring me the cream from the serving table. As you can see, I have my hands full at the moment."

Lucy sashayed to the table behind Lexie and fetched the pitcher for Alec, her ass cheeks barely covered by the sheer material of the miniscule apron. When she handed Alec the pitcher, she curtsied. "Anything else, Sir?"

"Pour it between her legs, Lucy, so the heavy cream mixes with her own sweet juices."

"Yes, Sir."

Never even looking at Lexie, she gently poured a healthy serving of cream down the woman's pussy. It was shockingly cold and Lexie gasped when Alec's hot tongue lashed out to lap it up. Her fingers tightened in his hair, pulling gently as her insides shook.

"Will there be anything else, Sir?" Lucy asked.

"I'm sure there will be. Please stand by the table and wait for my command." Alec looked up with hooded eyes, gazing at Lexie over her stomach. "Have you ever had anyone watch while you've been fucked?"

Lexie swallowed hard and licked her lips, her arousal spiking. Although she'd enjoyed a threesome in the White Room, noone had simply observed her getting fucked before, taking no pleasure of their own. Her body tingled with excitement.

Alec didn't wait for her to answer; he cleaned the rest of her with his tongue, the strawberry still balancing in her opening. He bit down on the fruit and slid it gently in and out with his mouth. Certain she was wet, he pulled the strawberry out slowly and stood, pushing two fingers deep inside. He popped the whole strawberry into his mouth, stem and all, and ate it, his eyes never leaving hers.

Her insides clenched around his fingers as he teased her to the brink. "You were even sweeter than the cream, Lexie," Alec said. "You're fucking delicious." He pulled his fingers from her and licked them, finishing every last drop of her.

"Lucy, come help me out of my tux," Alec said, even as he began unbuttoning his shirt. Lucy slowly removed his jacket and placed it over an arm as Lexie watched, eager to see what was beneath the form-fitting suit. He stepped out of his pants, wearing nothing beneath, and watched as both women's eyes widened in appreciation. Lexie wet her lips as he shrugged out of his shirt, his six pack straining as he twisted to hand Lucy his clothes.

"Thank you, Lucy," he said, her pout of disappointment satisfying Alec. "That will be all for now," he said, dismissing her.

Alec turned back to Lexie, catching her eyes appreciating his athlete's body. His grin was dark and delicious as he grabbed her legs and yanked her roughly to the end of the table so her bottom was dangling over the edge. Without any fanfare, he slammed deep inside, bottoming Lexie out. She was more than wet enough and screamed in pleasure as he pulled back out, pistoned softly at her swollen opening, and then slammed back inside, shoving so deep the table shifted back.

Lexie thrashed on the table, her body bucking against Alec's and matching his demanding pace. She was just on the brink of climaxing when Alec pulled out, pushing her body back up the table and making room for himself.

Lexie's eyes were clouded with lust when Alec called for Lucy again, having her pour the rest of the heavy cream all over Lexie's body and making a trail from her perfect breasts, down her flat stomach, and between her muscular thighs. He climbed onto the table and hoisted Lexie's legs back over his shoulders. Lexie moaned when Alec turned his head, slipping one of her sexy toes into his mouth and sucking hard on it while rubbing the pad of her foot.

"Ever been fucked on a dining room table, Lexie?"

Alec positioned his cock between her legs again, but didn't enter. He leaned over and licked the sweet cream from each of Lexie's breasts instead, taking a moment to bite and tug at her nipples as he had her toe. What could he say? He liked to lick things.

Lexie surprised him by lifting her head, tugging his lower lip into her mouth with her teeth. She bit gently before covering his mouth with hers, lapping the cream from his lips. Their tongues sparred, hers trying to set the pace. He grabbed her wrists and pushed them onto the table above her head, taking charge.

God it felt good to be the boss in the bedroom again. His half-grin was cocky, he knew. But it was justified as he slid the long length of himself back inside her. He knew with her legs up over his shoulders she would feel every inch. Alec continued to ravage her mouth, her hands still held captive above her head as he drove into her over and over again, her athletic frame rocking on the table each time their bodies collided. Her long nails dug deep lines down his back as she clenched around his cock and orgasmed, screaming as she came.

He slowed his pace to languid strokes as her body came down from its high, quivering beneath his weight. She lifted her lips, kissing his neck. "You haven't come yet," she said.

"I'm about to," he replied, sliding out and hopping off the table. He offered his hand, pulling Lexie to a seated position. She flushed bright crimson when she saw Lucy standing next to the side table, her eyes closed, her body nearly panting with desire from having watched them.

Alec wrapped his arms around Lexie's trim waist, squeezing and appreciating her plump bottom for the first time now that she was off the table. "Damn," he said, digging his fingers deep into one of her cheeks. He groaned. He was an ass man, and Lexie's was almost too good to be true.

He turned Lexie around in his arms, bending her over the table until her breasts were flat against the slick surface, forcing her to look at Lucy. He pulled her hands behind her back and placed his cock between her high, round cheeks, sliding it back and forth along her slick opening to get himself nice and wet. "You are to look at Lucy while I fuck you. Do you understand me, Lexie?"

Lexie nodded, pressing her ass against him, trying to invite him in faster. He pulled back. "I need you to answer me, Lexie, or you will not get my cock in your tight ass. Are we clear?" He rubbed the tip against her again. "Do you want me to fill you, Lexie? Have you ever had it this way before?"

"Yes, Sir, I have."

Alec grew harder, thinking of another man inside her ass.

"But I will enjoy it with you even more."

Alec leaned over and bit her shoulder hard before running his tongue along the slope of her neck. She pushed back, eager for him.

"And why's that?" he asked, placing his tip directly on her tight, puckered hole, preparing to enter her. He let go of her hands so he could spread her cheeks apart and watch as he took her.

"Because the only man who's ever had me there was my ex-husband," she admitted. "And there was no longer any pleasure when he took me. With you, I'm soaking wet and panting to have you slide inside me."

It was all he needed. He held her hips and entered, slowly at first. He didn't know how big her husband had been, but if there had been no pleasure, he assumed it wasn't big enough. Lexie groaned and pushed back, encouraging Alec to go farther. His heart pounded, wanting to devour and consume her fully. He kept one hand on her hip as he grabbed a fistful of her natural curls and pushed himself the rest of the way in, settling at the bottom so she could breathe and relax her insides around his cock.

"Are you ready?" he asked, gently swaying his pelvis as he slid back and forth. Her body rocked against his, never wavering. "Look at Lucy while I fuck you," he commanded, gently tugging her hair so her head raised to meet Lucy's eyes. Alec watched Lucy as she watched Lexie being fucked.

Lexie was ready for more. He grabbed both hips and pulled her to him with every thrust, pounding deep. What started as a few hard thrusts quickly turned to a toe-curling pace as he slammed into her as fast as he could. Lexie cried out and gripped the edge of the table as he plowed into her over and over again. It sent him over the edge. Three hard thrusts inside her impossibly tight ass later and he was done. An animalistic sound escaped his lips as he exploded, his body shaking against Lexie's tight, round ass.

He leaned over the table, his slick chest rubbing against Lexie's back. He circled her with his arms and cupped her breasts, massaging them as he licked the sweat off her shoulders. "God, you're fucking hot," he growled at Lexie.

She chuckled. "I thought I was sweet."

"Christ. You're that too," he said, laughing. He rose, helping Lexie stand, as well. He motioned to Lucy and asked her to bring him the tray of fresh berries and some more white chocolate. He wrapped one arm around Lexie's waist and dipped a strawberry in the warm chocolate for her, coating the base. "You are absolutely incredible, Lexie. Do you know that?" He placed the strawberry to her equally plump lips and pushed it in.

Her eyes never left his as she bit, savoring the sweet taste of chocolate and strawberries. She licked her lips as the juice ran over. "I do," she said, nodding.

Alec laughed. He appreciated a confident woman.

That's when he noticed a small tattoo running along her clavicle. It was a thin, delicate arrow with a fancy feather design at one end and "still I rise" in cursive along the arrow's shaft. *Indeed, she does,* Alec thought, admiring the strong woman before him.

"You promised I'd get a chance to taste something sweet from you," Lexie reminded him.

Alec asked Lucy to fetch a warm washcloth as Lexie dipped a finger into the bowl of white chocolate, bringing it to his mouth. She painted Alec's full lips before leaning forward to suck the chocolate off.

He knew their time was almost up, but he didn't care. He'd wanted to feel her lips around him from the moment he walked in and saw her lying on the table, her mouth a sinfully sweet dessert itself. When Lucy returned with the washcloth, he had her wash his cock off for him while he kissed Lexie, tugging and pulling at her bottom lip.

When Lucy was done, Lexie picked up the container and poured the remaining thick, warm chocolate over the tip of Alec's cock. He gasped when the heat of the liquid met his soft, clean skin. Lexie bent her knees and immediately took him into her mouth to sooth the pain with her wet tongue. The pleasure sent tidal waves of lust throughout his body. He'd never had anyone do that to him before, and the sensation was just as thrilling as he'd imagined it to be. He'd have to remember that for another day.

He pushed his hips forward and slid into her mouth, grabbing her soft curls as he did. She eagerly took him all the way in, sucking his shaft and the tip of his head like an ice cream cone she was sneaking on a hot summer's day. She cupped his ass and took him deeper into her throat, loving the soft texture of warm skin covering the hardness underneath.

"Lexie," he growled in warning, "I didn't think I'd come again so fast, but Jesus, your mouth is a wonderland." He slid in and out while holding Lexie's head in place, his eyes raising to meet Lucy's. He could tell she was hot with excitement, even though she was only allowed to watch.

His eyes never left Lucy's soft green ones as he fucked Lexie's mouth. He watched as she sucked the corner of her bottom lip in, biting it to remain neutral. Her body arched ever so slightly and Alec nodded, watching as relief washed over her face. She brought her hand down under the sheer skirt of her maid uniform and began to rub, even as Alec quickened his pace. Lucy closed her eyes, letting her head drop against the wall as she worked furiously. Alec was no monster. He knew she was going to need relief one way or the other after watching so dutifully today.

He raised a single finger to his lips and mouthed "Shhh" to her. Lucy nodded, parting her lips, her body shaking as she orgasmed silently, Alec's eyes never leaving her busy hand.

It was all he needed. He felt Lexie's teeth scrape against his shaft, sending shivers down his body as he exploded, bellowing out—this time with Lexie's warm tongue wrapped around him. She looked up at him with those stormy fucking eyes and grinned, raising to her feet and licking him from her lips.

"Delicious," she said, even as the bell chimed, signaling their time was over. Lexie ran her nails down his chest and to his waist, leaning in for one last kiss on her way out. "Thanks for showing me how sweet it could be, Sir," she said with emphasis. "And for making new memories to replace the old ones." She winked at Alec and sauntered out, her head held high, her large brown hair bouncing as she disappeared through the dining room doors—*like a boss*; he grinned.

Alec looked around at the mess and laughed. Strawberries, white chocolate, and rose petals covered the floor around the table as if there had been a massive food fight. He caught Lucy's eyes as he examined the carnage. Her chest heaved from her small release, but her eyes were aroused like a caged tiger in heat.

It was the least he could do . . .

"Follow me, Lucy," Alec said. He made a quick call to his concierge and led Lucy into the bathroom. If he had to shower anyway, he might as well have some fun doing it.

The warm water fell like a kiss from heaven over his tired frame. His body had taken a beating today on the court, and a sweet lashing while ravishing beautiful Lexie. As his muscles loosened under the hot spray, he pushed Lucy up against the shower wall, her hands pinned over her head. He pressed his new hard-on against her flat stomach and leaned forward, grabbing her earlobe between his teeth while biting down.

"You've been a very faithful servant, Lucy. It's time to receive your bonus," Alec said, dropping to his knees. He pushed her legs apart and inhaled deeply. She smelled like a warm cinnamon bun, and he couldn't wait to taste her.

God it's good to be the boss, Alec thought as he leaned forward and began his second round of dessert that day.

CHAPTER 10
CALLUM

C allum stretched out on the long white sofa like a lazy panther who had just finished bathing and was now luxuriating on a rock in the mid-afternoon sun. Rays of warm light streamed in to the White Room, but frosted windows hid the spectacular views of the city. One of the perks of the penthouse wasted, but for good reason.

Though, as Callum studied the frosted glass, a gleam came to his eyes as he imagined all the dirty ways he could pleasure his partner up against the cool surface of the tall glass windows. A cocky grin spread over his face as he rubbed his jawline, contemplating his options as he stroked his newly acquired beard.

The doors to the White Room opened and the blonde who sashayed through the opening nearly stopped his heart. Callum wasn't one for romance and fancy words, but she was literally like a ray of sunshine brightening the room even further. He took in the sleek, shoulder-length hair and the cute little bounce in her step. She was wearing nothing but a man's white dress shirt and a pair of black panties. Though one button held the shirt together at the center, he saw perfectly round tits beneath the crisp, white cotton. She was carrying an expensive camera in one hand, and fuzzy white handcuffs dangled from her wrist.

Callum was rarely at a loss for words, but he suddenly felt very, very parched. Luckily, the looker was also a talker.

"Mr. Davenport, I presume?" she asked, crossing the room to where he sat reclined. It wasn't his real last name, of course, but he nodded. She offered her hand and Callum was surprised when her shake was strong, firm, confident. "I'm here to take some press release photos of you today, at the studio's request. Shall we get started?"

This had to be her fantasy, because it sure as hell wasn't his. He yanked her by the hand, forcing her to sit on his lap and face him. Her brown eyes flashed hot with passion—or irritation—but she said nothing as she stared back at him. The rise and fall of her chest was the only sign that her heartbeat had quickened. In Callum's job, it was life or death to notice the details. He wanted to reach out and feel the thump-thump of her racing heart under his palm.

He focused on her words instead. "The studio got it wrong," he growled, his faint Scottish accent making him sound even more menacing. "I don't do photos." That's all Callum needed. Even if it was just for fun, there was no way in hell he could risk a real photo being taken with his profession.

He slowly slid his hand under the starched white cotton, dragging it up her bare side to the gentle curve of her breast. He didn't touch her fully, just traced his fingertips along her skin, teasing. "Why don't we switch roles and I'll take a few pictures of you, instead? Ever dream of being a pinup girl?"

She licked her lips, just inches from his. "I'm the photographer, not the model," she retorted. "But I suppose I could let you take one or two. You know, for your personal collection." She winked as she started to stand, but he yanked her back down, pushing into her with his hips as he settled her onto his lap. And his hard-on.

Callum ran his other hand along the side of her face, tucking a loose strand of hair behind her ear. Her skin was flawless, making him question just how young she really was. "What's your name, princess?"

She wrinkled her adorable nose. "I'm hardly a princess. I'm just here to do my job, Mr. Davenport. Then I'll be on my way."

Callum stood, lifting the woman on his lap with him. She wrapped her legs around his waist so she wouldn't fall, and he quite liked the feel of her warm center pressed against his bare stomach. "Drop the camera," he ordered. She scowled but conceded, letting the camera fall to the couch.

"If you're just here to do your job, then why do you have handcuffs?" He carried her across the room to the very window he'd been contemplating just moments ago. "And who are you?" he asked, pushing her back to the cool glass and pinning her.

"Who do you want me to be?" she challenged.

Callum dragged his eyes over her full lips, her straight white teeth, the dimple framing her saucy mouth. He wanted to take her chin in his mouth and suck on it. It was defiant, wealthy. You could always tell someone who came from money and those who did not. Callum fell into the latter category, but he saved every damn penny so he could fuck those who did.

"Summer," he said, pressing his muscular frame closer so they were now chest to chest.

"Cute," she said dryly. "Because I'm such a little ray of sunshine?"

Callum couldn't tell if she was playing the role or just being sarcastic. "No. Because I lost my virginity to a girl named Summer and you look just like her," he said, shutting her up. That part was true. And he'd never admit that she did, in fact, take over a room like a bright ray of sunlight. He'd lose his fucking mancard.

She ignored his retort. "So, why exactly do you have a problem with me taking your picture, Mr. Davenport?"

"Do you always talk this much?" Callum asked, snarling. He closed his mouth over hers to silence her. There was no way she was getting a picture, fantasy or not. As an undercover officer, he couldn't take that risk—it would ruin him.

Her tongue was quick, demanding. She tried to take control, drawing his thick tongue in and sucking it seductively as if it were something else. He'd give the hot little minx something to suck on later. She tugged at his lower lip before releasing it, running her mouth over his sexy, thick beard and down his neck.

"Enough!" he said, lowering her to the floor so he could remove the only thing he was wearing—his jeans. She stood against the cool, frosted glass, the white shirt now unfastened. Callum swallowed, nearly coming undone as he studied the curves of bare skin that peeked through. His eyes worshipped every inch of her body as he dropped his pants to the floor, kicking them to the side. He watched as Summer raked her eyes over his body, lust clouding her eyes as she made her way down.

"Summer," he whispered, leaning in, "you're in for a ride today. And you're not the one who's calling the shots, got it?" His hands went up and held both sides of her face as he kissed her, taking charge. Their tongues danced and jockeyed for alpha position, her hands going to his bare chest as the pace of their kiss quickened. He hoisted her back up so she was straddling his waist once again, her legs wrapping around his back.

"Callum—" she started, then quickly lost her thought when his hands slipped between her legs and slid her panties to the side. His fingers brushed her warm center, her viscousness telling him she was more than ready.

"I usually like a lot more foreplay than this, but ever since you walked through that door, I've been wanting to do this," he said. He guided Summer down his shaft, burying himself deep inside her. Instinctively, she wrapped her arms around his neck as he grabbed her ass, raising and lowering her back and forth on his cock. She ran her tongue up his neck and around the folds of his ear. *Jesus!* That was his weak spot. Not many women took the time to find it, let alone to zero in on it so fast.

She gasped when he plunged even deeper inside in slow, steady thrusts, his fingers digging into the soft flesh of her backside for leverage. "Do you like that?" he grunted, slowly pulling out. She locked eyes with him, nodding. "Then tell me," he said. "Tell me what you want."

She batted her mischievous brown eyes at him, cocking an eyebrow. "But—didn't you just silence me with your mouth?"

He pulled out and slammed back inside her, causing her to moan as her head fell back against the glass. Callum leaned over and licked along her collarbone, wanting so badly to get one of those perfect, puckered nipples in his mouth.

Get it together, man! Callum thought as he plunged deep inside her, riding her hard as she bounced up and down on his cock. At this rate, he wasn't going to last very long. And he wasn't a newb in the

White Room. What the heck was wrong with him today? It was as if he lost control the minute Summer strolled in, all that expensive blond hair shimmering in the afternoon sunlight. He pressed her back against the cool glass, one hand on her ass, the other flat against the wall by her head. He took a deep breath and slowed his pace, growling in her ear. "What the hell are you doing to me, blondie?"

Summer chuckled, low and sexy. "Yeah, this isn't going exactly how I planned either. Let me down, so we can slow this down. That's what was on the agenda today. A little role play, soft and slow."

Callum was confused, but he pulled out, lowering Summer to a stand. Her expensively manicured nails explored the flat planes of his stomach, over the sculpted ridges of his chest. "Wow," she breathed, stepping back. She ran a hand over her hair, smoothing it out. She was still wearing that sexy white shirt, but it was sliding off one shoulder now.

Summer lifted her gaze to meet Callum's intense scrutiny, her eyes flashing with heat as she stepped back, putting some distance between them. "Okay . . . let's slow this down and take this into the bedroom, shall we?"

"Why the bedroom?" Callum asked, stepping forward and brushing up against her body. He lifted his hands to her bare chest, noticing her nipple rings for the first time. He tugged one, watching as her eyes closed and her chest rose to meet his hands. "You like that?"

Summer nodded, swallowing. "I'm here to make you slow down,

Callum. You promised a previous client you would make love the next time, and she wanted you to see it through. This afternoon is on her. She insisted you let me take the lead and make love to you. I'm doing a pretty lousy job so far," she said, her laugh a little shaky.

"What did you just say?" Callum asked, stepping back and looking down at Summer, his alarm bells firing. "Why would you be talking to any client I've slept with? That's a huge breach of contract." A darkness crossed Callum's eyes as he considered the ramifications. "Has anyone else discussed this?" he demanded.

Summer shook her head. "Sorry, let me back up. Can we go to the bedroom though? I'd like a glass of wine and we can sit and talk before, well . . ." she trailed off, blushing, even though he'd just been buried deep inside of her. His cock tightened remembering the way she felt wrapped around him, but there was no more fucking till they got to the bottom of this.

He rubbed his beard, considering. Then nodded. It didn't matter where they talked, as long as she came clean.

When they entered the bedroom, he noticed a bottle of red and two glasses on the mirrored vanity. There was also a brush, a bottle of perfume, and makeup scattered over the surface. Summer poured the wine as Callum paced the room. He accepted his glass and took a healthy sip.

"Spill it," he said as Summer coolly sat down on the vanity's stool and gazed into the mirror.

She carefully removed the handcuffs from around her wrist and set them next to a row of makeup brushes. Summer lifted a bottle of Eros and applied a light spritz before picking up the brush. "Have you ever brushed someone's hair, Callum?" she asked, evading his question.

Callum took another sip and met her eyes in the mirror, narrowing them. In his line of work, he was a master at cuffing someone before they even knew what was happening. Even though these were just toys, he was tempted to wrap her hands behind her back, secure her with those damn fuzzy cuffs, and interrogate her hot little body with his tongue until she confessed.

"Come, brush my hair for me and I'll tell you what happened," Summer offered.

Callum rather liked his idea better, but he walked over and set his wine down next to hers. The white dress shirt was all but falling off, and he couldn't help but trail his fingers over her delicate shoulders. Her skin was softer than any he'd ever touched. *Jesus, she must be rich.* Without thinking, Callum ran his fingers over her thick wall of hair, lifting a soft strand and smelling it. *Yep, grapefruit.* He thought he'd smelled that earlier when he'd had her pushed up against the window.

Summer handed him the brush and asked, "Will you brush it for me while we talk?" Callum had something else in mind he'd rather do with the paddle brush. Something a little less intimate and intimidating. "It's okay, Callum. It won't bite."

He felt silly, but he reached out and ran the brush over her hair.

183

She closed her eyes and let out a sexy purr. Even though he just wanted answers, he'd do just about anything to hear her purr like that again.

"My real name is Arianna. Please don't share that outside this room. Names are still forbidden. I work for the White Room as the director of client experience. And my godmother owns the business now that her husband passed away."

Callum stopped brushing and met Arianna's eyes. "I'm sorry," he said. When she nodded quietly, he kept brushing.

"The woman you were last with is a regular client. After her time with you, she gave explicit instructions to her concierge, who passed them on to me. As the director, it fell into my purview. And . . ." Arianna trailed off, blushing. "Quite frankly, when I looked up your file and read the request, I wanted it for myself. I wanted you," she admitted.

Callum stopped mid-brush, his eyes meeting Arianna's in the mirror. "Why? It sounds like you could have anyone."

Arianna stood and turned to face him. "But I wanted you. Your profile, your passions, your drive . . . they mirror mine. And"—she lay her palms flat against Callum's chest—"you're pretty easy on the eyes," she said, grinning.

Callum brought his mouth to hers, crushing it. They were breathless by the time they both came up, chests heaving, raw heat flashing between them. "So you wanted to fuck me then, did you?" A predatory look flashed in Callum's eyes. He caught her hands in his own, dragging them down to his hardness. "Then fuck me."

She wrapped her hands around his width, slowly stroking him to an even bigger erection. "I said make love, my friend—not fuck. The instructions were clear. My client wanted to push you out of your comfort zone, see if you could let down some walls, she said."

Callum growled, remembering the sexy redhead she was referring to. He hadn't taken her request seriously, though he'd issued her a demand, as well. During their time together, she'd played the role of dominatrix with him. He rarely allowed that, but was glad he'd authorized it with her. She'd been soft but spunky, though not a true femdom. She had a long road ahead of her to really be comfortable in that role, but he loved being her first—and he could tell he had been. He hoped for her sake that she was keeping up her end of the bargain. Perhaps he'd see to it, he thought, grinning. Two can play at this game.

Callum turned his attention back to Arianna, taking her in. It was his lucky fucking day that she'd chosen to fulfill this fantasy with him. Going slow wasn't usually his thing, but he'd try just about anything once for this ballsy blonde.

"Then, by all means," he said, taking her hand, "make love to me."

Her breath hitched as electricity shot through their paired fingers. She swallowed, raising her eyes to meet his. A shared understanding passed between them, and lodged itself in Callum's belly—hot and unfamiliar.

Arianna leaned over, picking up the white handcuffs from the vanity. She crooked her finger in his direction as she made her way to the bed.

Callum arched a single brow. "I'm pretty sure handcuffs aren't a part of slow, passionate lovemaking." Not from his experience, anyway.

Arianna laughed as he followed her. "Says who? All the better to keep you in line with," she teased. "Otherwise, I don't trust you not to push me up against the wall and fuck the daylights out of me again."

Instant hard-on. "That's always a possibility," he said sheepishly.

Arianna tossed her blond silky hair over her shoulder as she glanced at him. Callum swallowed, his hand instinctively reaching out to caress her neck as he leaned in and inhaled. She smelled all soft and feminine, like flowers and citrus. He placed his lips on her neck for a long, slow kiss. She hummed as she relaxed into him. Callum covered her shoulders with kisses as he pulled her back against his chest. She still had far too many clothes on.

He reached around, dropping his hand inside those black silk panties, rubbing her mons as he sucked on the delicate flesh of her neck. Her hand followed suit, rubbing in sync with his fingers. He didn't know how much more he could take—going slow wasn't really his thing. He took the cuffs from her hand and tossed them to the bedside table before she could object.

Callum lowered the white dress shirt from her shoulders and

watched as it dropped to the floor. Her back was exquisite. A blank canvas of creamy white skin and lean muscle. He wrapped a hand in her soft blond hair and used the other to guide her facedown onto the bed until she was lying flat on her stomach.

Callum spread her legs open and massaged one of her ass cheeks, admiring the soft globes of her flesh. "Callum—" she moaned, low and throaty. This time when he silenced her with his tongue, it was on a different set of lips.

Holy hell she was sweet. Callum pushed Arianna's inner thighs higher, groaning when her legs slid up easily into a horizontal split before him. He grabbed his cock and began stroking. "Gymnast?" he croaked out.

"Cheerleader," she said, laughing.

"Christ," Callum whispered in awe, rubbing her ass as he buried his face between her legs. He would've devoured her under normal circumstances, but he gripped his cock, forcing himself to go slow.

His tongue darted out, tracing a line up one side of her hot center and down the other, loving the arc of her body as she pushed back to meet his mouth. He slid his nose up and down her glistening slit, making way for his tongue. She was like warm honey, thick and sweet as he plunged into her. He could eat her all day, but he was so swollen from lust he needed to feel her wrapped around his thick shaft. It would be so easy to push himself inside her from behind, keep her legs spread wide as he fucked her. But he was supposed to go slow, so he did.

He let her slowly ride his mouth, her hips rolling as she meet him stroke for stroke. He slipped a hand beneath her, finding her sensitive little nub. He knew it would be buzzing, ready. He rubbed it back and forth, applying just the pressure she'd need to see stars. It didn't take long. "Oh, God," she cried out, clutching the crisp sheets as she bucked against him. He rubbed her clit faster as he lapped his tongue up and down her sweet center. Her hole tightened as she pressed down, released.

Sighing with pleasure, she relaxed against Callum's mouth as he slowed his pace, lightly flicking her nub and causing her body to shudder as it slid into a satisfied afterglow. She rolled over like a pampered cat until she faced him, then scootched up farther on the bed until her head rested against the soft down pillows. "Get up here," she said huskily.

She rolled over, pulling a patented Sterling White condom from a porcelain container on the bedside table. Callum had used them with clients before, and they were like magic, barely perceptible on the skin.

He crawled up onto the bed, hovering his body just slightly above hers like a hungry cat stalking its prey. The look in her eyes was full of fire—and control. What a sexy fucking combination. Callum lay down, half of his body resting on her, the other half on the bed. They said nothing for a moment, just brown eyes meeting stormy blue ones.

Arianna reached up, running her hand over his face, tracing along his scruffy jaw in appreciation, and finding his lips. Her movements were so painfully delicious and slow. She pushed her finger into his mouth and watched as Callum took it in deep, sucking hard.

Callum ran his palm over her body, worshipping every dip and curve. He trailed his way down until he found her again, cupping her in his hand as he rubbed her, much slower this time. She arched into him, opening her legs for him. He groaned, covering her mouth with his. Her kiss was hot, demanding more. She grabbed his lower lip with her teeth and tugged, kicking his dick into overdrive.

Arianna gasped when he retaliated, slowly pushing two fingers inside of her, rubbing her pleasure spot deep within. Her hips arched, accepting them as deep as they would go. Callum nipped at her breast, taking her areola in his mouth and sucking it hard. She would have marks there in the morning, Callum knew. Love nibbles. He pulled at her nipple ring, tugging it to just the right limit before releasing, lapping the sensitive skin with his tongue. Her nipples were rock hard from arousal, her skin pebbling with goose bumps.

"Summer," he rasped, "I need to be inside you again."

Summer reached down, slowly rolling the condom on Callum with one hand. The soft trail of her fingers left him hard, wanting. She rolled onto her other side, pressing her firm bottom against him. Callum lifted her leg and slid deep inside, spooning her body as he rocked his hips back and forth. She arched back, opening her throat and mouth to Callum as he moved slowly, savoring the tight grasp she had around his cock.

"It's Arianna," she moaned. "I want to hear you say my real name when you make love to me."

"Jesus, Arianna," he groaned. He kissed her neck as he ground himself slowly, deeply inside her. They found a deliciously tantalizing pace of meeting each other partway, the deep thrust and bottoming out binding them. It wasn't enough.

Callum rolled Arianna onto her back so she could look up at him. If he was going to make love to her, she sure as hell was going to look him in the eyes when he did. He found her soft opening and pressed inside, his gaze never leaving hers. She parted her legs farther and arched her hips up, guiding him as he buried himself in her sweet depths. Though his strokes were slow, he meant business. It was as if he couldn't get deep enough, close enough to Arianna. He wanted her in ways he couldn't name.

She rolled her eyes closed, moaning as he ground his hips against hers. "Is this slow enough, love?" he growled.

He didn't give her time to answer. This time he pulled almost all the way out and plunged back deep inside in one swift, hard thrust. Her body bounced back as he bottomed her out. Her lips parted on instinct, biting the lower corner as she moaned. "God, Callum!"

It was too much, he had to have her. His lips found hers,

searching, demanding as he slid slowly back and forth. Their tongues pushed and circled, heating Callum from the inside. He dropped to his forearms so he could cup her face, biting her lower lip as he quickened his pace. Arianna gasped, wrapping her legs around his waist to pull him in as deep as he could go.

"Look at me, Arianna," Callum said, dropping soft kisses to her lips as he drove her to the edge. She took his breath away when she looked up at him through her thick lashes, her velvety brown eyes melting something frozen deep inside his core. "I want you to come with me," he said. "Are you close?"

Arianna dug her nails in his back in response, her eyes rolling closed as her body shook against his. She was still trembling when he slammed deep within her for his final three thrusts, coming hard as her name tumbled from his lips.

He collapsed against her, resting his head in the crook of her shoulder. "God you are sexy," he said, his voice muffled in her hair. "I don't know if that was slow enough for you, but it sure felt like making love," he said, without thought.

Her hand stilled on his lower back when he said it. He could feel her breath hitch. She said nothing, though, as she kissed his shoulder, her fingers resuming their soft dance over his back.

He pushed himself up, rising to a stand as he stretched out the long length of his body. God, he felt limber and satiated. He grinned down at her, seeing the fire still in her eyes. He discarded the condom in the small trash bin under the bedside table, noticing the cuffs he'd tossed there earlier.

"Sorry I never let you use the handcuffs," Callum said, laughing. Absently, he picked them up and dangled them from his finger. "Usually I'm the one putting them on, not the other way around," he admitted. Though she likely knew that if she'd read his profile.

"It's not too late," she whispered, reaching up to snatch them from his hand. She laughed, falling back against the pillow just as the gentle chime rang out from above.

"Fuck!" Callum frowned, not ready for his time with Arianna to end. He didn't believe in love at first sight, but there was something special about her that told him their story wasn't over yet.

"Since you work here, can I see you again?" Callum asked. He knew the answer would be no, but two hours had been nowhere near enough time with this spunky, heated woman. They hadn't even touched the tip of the iceberg together, he could tell. He hardened just thinking of all the ways he still wanted to take her—all the dark, delicious secrets he could show her.

Callum searched the room for his pants, remembering they were in the living room. He was on his way out to get them when she answered him quietly.

"Actually," she said, fingering the fuzzy white cuffs, "it's funny you ask."

He turned, his body half in and half out of the bedroom.

Callum's fingers dug into the door frame.

"Avaline, my godmother, just recently changed the rule after a unanimous vote by the board."

He turned, his body fully facing her, but not moving an inch to go back inside—yet.

"What?" he growled.

"Clients will soon be able to request a former lover. If the other person agrees, they can be matched any time the pair requests it. She's also reducing the time allowed between visits for platinum clients to once every four weeks."

Callum ran a hand down over his face. It wasn't enough. It was a start, but it would never be enough with Arianna.

He stalked toward her, a dark, brooding look crossing his eyes as he took her in, white, silky skin against white, silky sheets. "And what if that's not enough?" he demanded.

He watched as Arianna swallowed, licking her lips. Her chest heaved, no words spoken. She rose to her knees, crooking her finger at him again. He'd been told to slow down once; he had no intention of doing it again anytime soon. He wanted Arianna twenty ways to Sunday.

"That's at the client's discretion," she said, slowly.

He stood in front of her, his hand reaching up behind her neck to grab the back of her head. He took the handcuffs from her hand, trailing the soft fur down her chest from her neck to the flat, taut lines of her stomach. Her body twitched in pleasure. She closed her

C.M. ALBERT

eyes as he trailed them up her body again.

He leaned forward, his mouth to her ear. "This is definitely not over between us then, Arianna. But you'll have no other while we're fucking," he said, backing up and pinning her with his eyes. "Do you understand? I won't share you with anyone else."

"You've shared before," Arianna replied coyly. "Isn't that the idea of the White Room, after all?"

Dark heat rolled through his veins. "That was before you," Callum said. "Now it isn't good enough."

"After one afternoon?" she pressed.

"After one afternoon. Hell . . ." he said, raking his hand over his head. "I knew you were trouble the minute you walked through the door with a freaking camera." He laughed, glad she'd forgotten all about that.

"I'd like that, Callum," she said low, almost making him doubt if he heard her right.

"Which part?" he pressed, his hand going into her hair again, pulling her head closer to his so their eyes locked.

Her lips parted, sexy as fuck. He wanted to feel them wrapped around him. He wanted so many things with her. Most of all . . . he wanted to know more about her.

"All of it. But not in the White Room. If you want my body exclusively—as I'd have yours—no money can be exchanged. I told you I wanted you from the first time I read your profile, and I wasn't kidding. I chose you for a reason."

Callum swallowed, his cock tightening. It was more than that though. She stirred something within him that had long ago closed. For the first time in a long while, he had hope. Arianna was a beautiful woman. One he could fuck dirty and one he could make slow, passionate love to. One whom he wanted to snuggle up with on the sofa and eat cereal with in the morning out of the same bowl. And one he wanted to spread up against the window again and lick until she screamed out his name.

His mouth met hers, taking her slowly, with the confidence of knowing he'd get to see her again, and not a desperate last kiss to hold him over until his next encounter in the White Room with another stranger. God that sounded good. Something he never even realized he wanted.

He pulled back, knowing their time together had ended for the day, the chime long ago over. "I can't wait to see you again," he said, resting his forehead against hers.

"Who said anything about next time?" she asked.

When confusion crossed Callum's face, she laughed. "I just meant, I'm not done with you yet today."

Relief flooded his body. She dangled the handcuffs from her hand and stood, walking slowly toward the living room. "Are you coming?" she asked, her shiny blond hair swinging gracefully over her shoulders.

"There's a desk chair I have a mind to cuff you to," she said before walking from the room.

Callum closed his eyes, images of what she would do to him in that chair flashing through is mind. He wasn't sure how he got so lucky. He'd walked into the White Room not knowing what awaited him sexually. Now, when he walked toward Arianna and the pleasure they were about to share, he knew exactly what to expect—and it was mind-blowing.

It was what lay ahead for his heart that he was unsure of now. He had a feeling he was a goner.

Hell, he already was.

CHAPTER 11
BARON

Baron James hadn't returned to the White Room since his visit with Arianna. The naughty minx had shown up to his Sunday service wearing a demure lace dress that was far sexier than the little hair dresser getup she'd worn the last time he'd seen her. The corner of Arianna's mouth twitched as Avaline introduced her goddaughter to Baron after church, asking if he'd like to join them for brunch. Arianna had entirely too much pleasure watching him squirm his way out of that one.

But the White Room called to him. His triathlon was over and he needed an outlet for the excess energy he had coursing through his veins. The church fulfilled his heart, replacing the romantic love he'd lost after the death of his beloved Sarah. But the White Room fulfilled other needs that he wasn't willing to share outside of these sacred walls. As a pastor, he couldn't easily engage in an open relationship without strings. And his heart was nowhere near ready for strings again.

The White Room was the answer to his prayers. Safety. Reliability. Anonymity.

Heat.

So much heat he had inside. Pastor or not, he was a man first. And the White Room helped him remember that side of himself. One that was kept caged ninety percent of his life, until he needed relief. Avaline, being a regular church member again after Henri's passing, had informed him that some of the rules had changed in the White Room. Platinum guests were now allowed visits every four weeks, and repeat visits with past clients upon request. While his time with Arianna had been hot—hotter than Baron usually allowed—seeing someone more than once felt too much like the beginning of attachment. And the church was the only attachment he had room for in his heart.

It had been much longer than six weeks since his last visit, and the heat inside Baron had been building for far too many months. Arianna had encouraged him to expand his boundaries in the White Room, though Baron resisted the idea every moment since his last encounter.

Until today.

Today, his boundaries were for the taking. And the woman who would help him expand his horizons would be gentle, yet firm, he was told. Safety, even with the heat. Especially with the heat.

When he opened the door to the White Room, he wasn't sure what to expect. But it wasn't the beautiful redhead whose electric green eyes pierced his own from across the room. Elegant, but sexier than sin, was an understatement. She stood next to the fireplace, a long, leather riding crop in her hand. Baron swallowed hard as his eyes traveled over her body from head to toe. A demur, white silk blouse was tucked neatly into a black waist corset cinched tightly over a long, black, tight-as-hell pencil skirt. Long, thin legs wrapped in lacy high heels added a good three inches to the vixen.

Though her blouse was demure, the way it gaped open from corset to oversized pussycat bow was not. The long, ruffled bow secured at her throat was far sexier than almost anything else she was wearing. It brought images of a naughty librarian to mind. Perhaps the sexy, low bun in her hair helped reinforce that image too. But it wasn't a librarian she was playing today. No librarian he'd ever met carried a riding crop like that.

He walked in, exactly as he'd been instructed. He said nothing as he crossed the room toward her. He'd been told to sit at her feet and wait for instructions. But he wasn't sure he could do that—even to stretch his own boundaries.

His mouth was dry as his eyes ran up her long, lean legs. When Baron got closer, he noticed a sexy little mole at the corner of her mouth. In her heels, they were almost the same height, and for some reason that turned him on to no end.

"Sit," she commanded, pointing the crop to the floor in front of her. Baron had had no intention of complying, but the way she said it—with authority and heat racing together—made him suddenly want to please her.

When he kneeled in front of her, she stepped closer, lifting his chin so their eyes met again. "I'm told you are new at this type of game play, so I will be gentle. To a point. Do we understand each other?"

Baron swallowed, but nodded. "What should I call you?" he asked. This was so different from his time with Arianna, but he grew hard imagining what might come next. He had no context to draw on that would suggest what she could possibly have in store for him.

"You may call me Wendy. Though I usually like my partners a little younger, I'm excited to bring a mature man over to the fun side. Most younger men are easy to please and train, but bringing a real man to his heels and hearing him beg is even more satisfying," she said as she trailed the leather crop over his bare chest. He'd been instructed to wear only black jeans into the room.

"And what shall I call you?" she purred, smacking him lightly on the back with the padded leather end of her crop. It was light, hardly detectable, but stung enough at the end to send a sharp pain of lust straight between his legs. *Hmmm . . .*

"You can call me Gael," he said, giving her his middle name. She looked him over, from his salt-and-pepper, graying copper hair to the freckles that lined his naked, chiseled chest.

"We have something in common then," she said. "I, too, am Irish."

Baron smiled, feeling a little more relaxed. Until she thwapped him on his ripped abs with the riding crop, using a little more intensity than before. He steeled himself, showing no signs of the pain that lit up his nerve endings.

"So, you are new to this. Are you open for anything I desire today, or are there limitations?"

Baron looked up at her, still on his knees. He was so close to her he could practically smell her female scent. He wanted so badly to reach out and run his hand up her long, thin leg to her hot center. He wanted to know what she was wearing underneath, and whether she, too, had freckles hidden beneath the silk.

"There are limitations, but I'll let you know if we hit a boundary when I get to it. I know my desires and how deep they run, but I also know my heart. I will never do anything I feel degrades either one of us. Or causes real pain. I am someone who brings love into this world, nothing else. So as long as our play is consensual and sensual, I'm in."

Vironica nodded, understanding and respecting his lines. They were her own, after all. She went deeply sensual and on the edge, but nothing that crossed the line and lost sight of the woman she really was.

"We are on the same page then. Are you open to a little spanking, or a little pain?" she asked, curious.

Lust seared him, but frightened him too. "To a point," he said honestly.

"Understood. Well, I have a surprise for you today, but we will warm up out here first. Since you are already on your knees, you are in the perfect position to eat me, are you not?" She placed one of her high heels onto the raised fireplace ledge and placed a hand to Baron's head, her fingers lacing in his hair.

Baron ran his hands up the outside of her legs. They were so soft, so long. He gently slid the pencil skirt up, in sync with his hands as they ventured up to her trim hips. They hadn't even kissed yet, but Baron found himself leaning in, taking a whiff of her luscious core. She was wearing a white lace thong, barely covering an inch of her. He noticed she was bare and smooth, a smattering of freckles across her lower abdomen. He wanted to taste her, but the stupid thong was in his way.

Baron reached up and ripped the panties, tearing in opposite directions until the material snapped, freeing his access to her. He dropped them to the floor and leaned in, stretching his tongue out for a first swipe at her clit. It was hard, and larger than he expected. She smelled like heaven—an earthy, floral scent that reminded him of the wisteria Sarah used to keep in the house. He felt like it was a sign. As if she were giving him permission to be here, to move on.

He dove into Wendy with abandon, wrapping his arms around her legs and burying his face in her sweet opening. Her legs were parted, giving him full access to her center. As he lifted his mouth to meet her, he felt just how wet and sweet she really was. It was like lapping fresh summer cream. He grasped her ass, pulling her center closer to his mouth. His tongue darted up into her hot opening, lunging as deeply as he could while rubbing his nose along her sensitive nub.

Wendy responded by grasping his hair tighter, moaning as he pushed his face even closer, helping her ride his mouth to orgasm. Her body released like a string that snapped after being wound too tightly. She shook, her legs tightening around his head as she came. Baron buried his face even deeper, not letting go until her body released several mini-orgasms, not unlike the aftershocks of an earthquake.

"Mmm," she purred, lowering her leg from the fireplace.

"Not yet," Baron growled, standing. He would let her call most of the shots, but he wasn't done with her yet. He lowered his hand and played with her clit again, this time with his fingers. He watched as her eyes widened, then closed as warm waves of pleasure washed over her.

"Oh, that's nice," she said, opening her leg back up to let him in. He rubbed his fingers along her slick entrance.

"You are so wet," he said in awe. He leaned forward, taking her neck in his mouth and sucking it hard. Her skin was flawless, pale. She had a few freckles on the side of her neck, under her ear. He ran his tongue up her throat, taking her earlobe in his mouth and biting as he inserted two fingers deep inside her below.

"Oh God, yes," she breathed. He thrust his tongue inside her ear, lapping at the gentle folds as he rubbed his fingers in and out of her tight opening.

"Do you like this?" he asked, cupping her chin in his hand, forcing their eyes to meet. A heat and comfort shot strait to his cock as they stared, a knowing he didn't understand coursing through him. Sparks of heat flew from that single glance, had her panting in time with his fingers.

"Wendy," he said, slowing his pace, unsure of the feelings racing through him. Feelings he'd only felt once before in his life. Feelings that scared the fuck out of him.

She placed both hands on the sides of his face, leaning in for a kiss. Her lips were soft, so soft, on his own. Like coming home. "Don't stop, Gael. Please don't stop what you're doing." Her lips closed over his, taking his tongue deep inside, their mouths dancing in unison as if they'd kissed a thousand times before.

Gael moved his fingers deep inside her, finding her sacred space and running his fingers back and forth as she tightened around him in pleasure. "Like this?" he asked, coming up for breath. "Is this what you want?" He plunged his fingers deeper, then almost pulled them back out, playing with her wet opening and clitoris before plunging them back deep inside, setting an intoxicating rhythm.

"Yes! Oh God, yes!" she cried out. She bit his lower lip as he moved his fingers in and out, helping her ride another wave of orgasm. Her legs shook, her thighs clasping his hand as he worked his magic to help her come again.

He slowed his fingers as she rode out her pleasure, little tremors shaking her body against his, her head resting on his shoulder.

"Mmm . . ." Baron said, removing his fingers from her core. She pulled back and straightened her pencil skirt. He knew his hair was mussed from her fingers. He didn't care. "Dear God, you are like summer honey, fresh from the hive," he said. "Here, taste yourself," he said, offering her his finger.

Hesitation had her pausing, but she opened her mouth, letting him slide one of his slick fingers into her mouth. His eyes never left hers as she suckled his finger, her coral lips cupping him like it was her last meal and food had never tasted so good. He growled. "Perhaps it's time for you to kneel, Wendy."

Lust brightened her eyes. "Free me from my clothes first, Gael," she said.

Baron slowly untied the prim-and-proper bow at her neck, the silk soft and inviting against his skin. He rubbed the material between his fingers, Wendy noticing the look of heat filling his eyes.

"You like that, don't you?" she said.

"I do," he admitted. "It feels like the creamy softness of your thighs."

Wendy swallowed, licking her lips as he unclasped the single button. He lifted the tails of her blouse from the corset at her waist, freeing the material from its trap. She helped Baron remove the blouse from her petite frame, exposing small, high breasts for his inspection.

"They're not very big," she said, "but they're highly sensitive."

Baron ran his fingers over her tiny breasts. They were small because she was thin, hardly any fat on her. Despite her age—Baron suspected they were nearly the same number of years—her breasts pointed up, like sweet cones tipped with a big cherry. His palm fit neatly over her breast, his fingers massaging her tight nub between his fingers. Her body shook in response. He rolled it back and forth between his fingers, watching her body arch and push against his in response. His cock tightened, enjoying just how sensitive her breasts really were. God, he couldn't wait to taste them later. But first . . .

He unlaced her black leather corset, tossing it to the floor. Then Baron unzipped her long, black pencil skirt, holding her hand so she could step out of it in her strappy high heels. She stood before him in only pearls and heels. He was harder than he'd ever been.

"Tell me what you want, Gael," she said.

Baron growled, guiding her head down as she dropped to her knees in front of him. The fire was warm against his ass, and nothing was a prettier sight than seeing her kneel in front of him, all prim and proper. He reached out, pulling her bun free and gasping as long, copper waves spilled out over her shoulders.

"Suck me," he growled, his hands going to all that luscious hair. She lifted her silk blouse and ran it between his legs, holding one end in front of him and the other from behind. She very slowly slid the silk blouse between his thighs, letting the silk rub gently over his balls. He groaned, rubbing himself against the silk as it swiped back and forth along his skin, sending spears of heat straight to his belly.

She was on both knees when she lifted the silk from between his legs, wrapping it around his wide cock. She stroked up and down with it, letting the silk massage Baron's length as her nimble fingers danced in time with the movement. The cool silk and the warm fire was nearly too much. Or so he thought. Until she wrapped her warm mouth over him. The silk shirt dropped to the floor as her mouth received him—all of him—taking him deep inside her throat. Baron groaned as he pumped into her mouth, her tongue swirling around him with each thrust. He wouldn't last if she kept that up with her wicked little tongue. While he would love to come inside her mouth, he wanted more. He *needed* to feel himself inside her.

"Get up!" he said, helping pull her to a standing position.

She pouted prettily. "I was enjoying myself."

"You'll enjoy it even more when I spread your legs apart and bury myself deep inside you; I promise you that." He cupped the back of her head, pulling her in for a kiss. His five o'clock shadow left a rosy glow on her cheeks and chin when they parted. He loved knowing he caused that, and he couldn't wait to leave some chafe marks on her beautiful tits too.

"You said you had a surprise for me?" he asked.

She nodded, taking his hand and leading him from the living room.

"If it involves me being inside of you, then I'm all for it."

"Oh, you'll be inside of me, all right," she said, her tight ass flexing with each step as she led him by the hand. She slid open the large doors that led to the dining room, though all the furniture had been removed. In its place was a large, black contraption that looked like a swing set, leaving Baron really confused.

"And this would be . . ." he said, trailing off at a loss for words.

"Your biggest sexual fantasy you never knew you had," she answered.

Baron had no idea what it did or how they would use it, but as an adrenaline junkie, it certainly piqued his interest. There were all kinds of ropes hanging from the device, and it both intrigued and terrified him. "As long as my limits are respected," he said, uncertain.

She laughed, deep from the throat. "Don't worry, it's not as scary as it looks. Here," she said, walking over, "it is nothing more than a sex swing and harness. You or I can get into hundreds of different positions with this, and it helps support our weight so we can be more adventurous and try new things. If we want a little momentum, we have it. If you want a little tension, we have it. The world's our oyster with this," she breathed out, her nipples hard and excited as she grasped one of the poles that kept the contraption standing upright.

Baron leaned over and finally took one of her nipples in his mouth, sucking hard. Her skin was just as soft and sweet at he knew it would be. "So tell me how to get you into this thing, because I'm getting impatient," he said.

"How do you want me? That determines how I set it up." She turned, looking coyly at him over her shoulder. "Do you like me like this, doggy style? Or . . ." She bent all the way down, grasping her ankles and leaving herself open to Baron. Her ass spread perfectly, her delicious pink center teasing and inviting. He couldn't help but lean over and lick up her hot opening in appreciation. "Like this?"

"Yeah, I kinda like seeing you like that," he growled, taking himself in his hand and stroking.

She rose, tossing her hair back as she did, the curls bouncing against her back. "And so it will be," she said, adjusting the harness. "Come," she said.

She leaned over a large padded strap, her stomach resting on it. Grabbing the pole in front of her with both hands, she pulled herself forward. "Place my knees in those stirrups," she instructed Baron. His cock tightened as he saw her nearly bent over, the harnesses dangling, waiting for her knees.

He walked up behind her, stroking her ass and admiring the view. God she was beautiful. Freckles were generous along her thighs, and he was torn between wanting to bury his face between her legs again and fucking her from behind.

"Hurry, Gael," she said. "I am dying to feel your thick cock fill me up."

It was suddenly easy to make his decision. He hoisted her knees into the stirrups, one after the other, and felt so much power and so much need course through him as he saw her spread out before him, eager for him to take her.

He ran his fingers delicately over a single cheek, then massaged it, rolling the muscle between his fingers.

"Oooh, I like that," she said. "Have you ever spanked someone?"

He remembered his time with Arianna. She had spanked him once or twice, but he had never returned the favor.

"I haven't," he said honestly. But staring at her porcelain, freckled ass made him want to more than ever. He swallowed. "But I want to. Man, I want to," he said, stroking himself.

"Then do it, Gael. This is about stretching your limits, getting out of your comfort zone. I like it. It's mutual. It brings me pleasure. So, I want you to spank me while you fuck me."

She looked over her shoulder, her red hair tumbling over her trim back. He couldn't wait any longer to be inside her.

He pulled her forward by the waist and stood between her outstretched knees. He slid inside slowly, savoring her tight pussy as she adjusted to the width of him. She moaned every time he pushed a little farther. When he was buried all the way in, balls deep, he slapped her ass. It jiggled against his stomach, her pussy tightening around the length of him. The bright pink spot on her ass caused him to tighten, pushing deeper still.

She screamed out, bucking against him.

"Is that okay? Did that hurt?" he asked, uncertain. The look she gave him over her shoulder was one that was wild, uninhibited.

"God, no, Gael. I want more," she panted. "Use the harness to push me and pull me, like a swing."

He nodded, grabbing the harness at her waist and pushing her forward as he pulled his cock back. He soon created a gentle rhythm, helping her bounce easily along the length of him. She was so wet it became apparent she could bounce right off him, then glide right back on. He found himself increasing the distance and letting her truly swing forward, then come back and slide back down his cock. The sight was heady to have her so open to him, so pliable as he slid in and out.

The last time she came back to him, he steadied her, then smacked her ass again, enjoying the skin pink up as it smarted from his hand. Her cheeks jiggled in response and she tightened around him.

"Are you ready?" he asked. When Wendy nodded, he grabbed the strings of her waist harness and held on, using the tension to keep her still while burying himself as far as he could go.

He pounded into her, over and over, her back arching as she bucked against him with every thrust. He wasn't sure he'd ever been so deep inside someone before. He let go and reached around, cupping her tiny breasts and pinching her nipples, his back covering hers as he set a frantic pace to the end. Their bodies were slick with sweat by the time they were ready to climax. He stood up, grabbing her long red hair in his hand and pulling her head back. He loved the waist harness that kept her in place, secured her, let him focus on their orgasm and not supporting their weight.

He pumped hard several more times until he felt her tighten around him, her insides growing wetter as her entire body trembled from her orgasm. He wasn't far behind. A few more deep and rapid strokes had him pulling out, releasing himself onto her back. He reached out, rubbing the warm liquid over her soft skin.

After Baron helped her down from the harness, he pulled her to him, their bodies mingling as closely as their breaths. He kissed along her neck, to her ear, across her cheek, until he found her mouth. "God, Wendy . . ." He couldn't find the words. She had made him feel safe, and he felt freer than he ever had.

"I know," she breathed. "That was unbelievable."

"Is it always like that with the swing?" he asked.

"I don't know," she admitted. "That was my first time, too." Her cheeks flushed prettily.

The chime rang out, signaling their time was over. Two hours hadn't been enough time. He closed his eyes, suddenly sad to say goodbye to this beautiful woman.

"Wendy," he said, "that was something more for me. I . . . I felt things today with you that I haven't in a long time."

His eyes met hers, looking for something he wasn't sure he was searching for. Until he found it.

"I know," she whispered. "It was more than just sex, today, wasn't it? You felt it too?" she asked, sounding almost shy.

He nodded. "I wish there were more time." He'd never really wanted that before, or another go with the same woman. He loved the once-and-done approach to the White Room. But suddenly, he wanted more. "Shit!" he said, heading out to grab his jeans. He slid them up his trim waist, fastening them.

He turned to look at Wendy, in all her trim sexiness, wearing nothing but heels. She'd followed him into the living room and was standing jauntily against the stately white doors to the bedroom. "Rules are made to be broken, Gael," she said.

His heart was torn between desire and safety. Between his past and something so completely wild, fresh, and vulnerable.

"Actually, I was told by the owner that we can request past lovers now," he said hoarsely. He was both looking for her reaction and hedging himself, unsure if he could take this big of a leap with his heart.

"So I've heard," she said, the corner of her mouth curling into a smile. She strolled over to him, completely confident in her own skin. Her long red curls soft against her beautiful, naked skin.

He wanted more time with her. He did. So why was opening his heart so damn hard?

She placed her hands on his sculpted chest, trailing them down his stomach to the waist of his jeans. She gave a gentle tug, pulling him closer. She leaned in, brushing his ear with her lips.

"I will wait for you, Gael. I see the war in your eyes. I can tell you've been hurt. When you are ready, you let the White Room know. I will wait only for you before coming back."

Baron's heart flooded with emotions. He searched Wendy's eyes, connecting far deeper than their bodies just had. "It's Baron," he said. "Baron Gael James."

She nodded, smiling. "Vironica," she whispered.

Baron grinned, his dimples flashing. He realized he was truly happy for the first time in a long while.

"I'll be back for you, Vironica. Give me a little time to get used to the idea. My heart's been broken before, and I never knew it could open again—not like this." He ran a hand along her cheek, cradling the side of her face as he kissed her slowly, deeply.

"You stirred something that I thought was dead inside of me, Vironica. Let me battle my demons. Heal. Then I'll be back for you. I promise. And I don't make promises lightly," he said, lifting his finger to the sky.

Vironica didn't know just how deep his promise ran, but she couldn't wait to see him again. She returned his kiss one last time and walked away, leaving the White Room.

Baron had come in one man, and was leaving with the hope of something completely new. It terrified him to his bones. But nothing scared him more at that moment than never seeing those green eyes again.

He would be back. Come hell or high water, he would possess Vironica again. This time winning her heart as well as her body.

CHAPTER 12
RAINE

Adelaide went by Raine in the White Room. She could've gone by Addie—the nickname most people called her. But Adelaide Eckleberry was such a distinct name, and the one thing she prized the most about the White Room was the anonymity it provided. It wouldn't do to have WLNC's morning anchor caught up in a scandal of her own. Though many of the city's top one percent knew about the White Room, it was very much on a hush-hush basis. It only survived because it was kept that way. With strict rules. Rules Adelaide needed if she wanted to keep her job. And her trust fund.

But thanks to her very connected friend Arianna from Wells

Media, she had a lifetime key to the White Room. She didn't know how Arianna got her in, but she was grateful for it; and she knew Arianna had a lifetime pass, as well. They would often swap stories over after-work drinks about their more memorable sexcapades— some were too good not to giggle over. But sometimes a girl had to keep certain dark proclivities even to herself.

Today was one of them.

Adelaide was dressed in a pair of black miniscule booty shorts made for exercising. A small white sports bra loosely covered by a gray open-sided, sleeveless hoodie completed the look. The vibe said sexy-sporty—not complete tramp. She'd pulled her long blond and brown balayaged hair into a high ponytail, and her nude makeup and long lashes left her looking like the fresh-faced girl next door that she was.

Just a girl next door with a crazy hot fantasy she never dreamed she'd have the balls to live out. Until the White Room. Until now.

She was finally ready.

She thought.

I am ready, aren't I?

Adelaide did a few hops on the balls of her toes, stretching her calves and trying to shake the jitters. It was too late. The large double doors to the White Room opened, and in walked two of the most handsome men she'd ever seen. Adelaide was suddenly very unsure if she could go through with this.

The man on the left was muscular, but leaner than the one on the right—though in a sexy, American Ninja Warrior kind of way. Mixed with a little Abercrombie & Fitch, all spiky beach-blond hair and ice blue eyes. *Holy hell.* The scruff along his angular jaw left Adelaide panting for how that would feel scraping along her thighs.

Okay . . . so maybe this was a good idea, afterall. Adelaide grinned, suddenly eager to start the "workout session" she had booked with her two "fitness trainers."

The man on the right looked like he could be brothers with the other guy. But he was a lot more muscular in an I-pump-weights-at-the-gym-every-day kind of way. And his brown hair and tattoos set him apart. A large Celtic-inspired cross flanked his huge bicep on his right arm, while a large Chinese symbol for strength was etched on his other bicep. Adelaide knew because she had the same tattoo on her rib cage, close to her left breast—though for very different reasons, she suspected. He, too, had a face full of scruff, and Adelaide's panties grew damp just imagining all the ways these guys might want to work her out today.

"Hey," said blondie, reaching out his hand to Adelaide. "I'm Anders, and this toad is my brother, Ari. We were told you needed some personal trainers. . . to work some really hard-to-reach spots?" he said with a wink.

Adelaide tried really hard not to roll her eyes, but she couldn't help it. She muffled her laugh, though, so it ended up sounding like a stifled cough. She wasn't sure how she would ever get through this with a straight face.

"Hi, Anders. Ari," she said, reaching her hand out to accept Anders's firm grasp. He was confident, the cocky one. She could tell straight away by his sun-kissed, frosted hair to his blue lagoon eyes, which were pinning her now, raking up and down her legs, her booty shorts hiding absolutely nothing. She tugged at one of the hems absently, not sure what to do with her hands now. She waved to Ari, who stood in the background, a dark, brooding look in his eyes. While Anders kicked her libido right in the gut and made her sit up and take notice, Ari's simmering sexiness was like a slow boil.

"Uh, so you guys are really brothers? Or . . . you know. Just for today?" *Stupid, stupid, stupid!* Adelaide thought. But they *did* look an awful lot alike; it made her curious.

"We're actually brothers," Anders said, surprising her. "I got all the looks in the family. I'm one of five boys. Ari has a few years on me. But he's a still a good trainer," he added.

Adelaide let her gaze cascade appreciatively over Ari's body. He was much bigger than Anders, but not in a meathead kind of way. More in an I-can-bench-press-your-entire-body-which-is-sexy-as-fuck kind of way. Adelaide didn't know where or whom to start with. She wanted them both.

"So . . . this is a little awkward," she started. "I've—eh-hem—never been trained by two men before, if you know what I mean," she said, blushing.

Ari finally spoke, his eyes gentle. "It's okay. We've never trained the same woman together before, so we're all new to this. And, before you ask . . . no. We are not going anywhere near each other. Our focus is on you. You're the client. You get all the attention."

Oh. Gulp.

Adelaide peered through her lashes at Ari. Though he seemed to be the quieter one, he was doing all the right things to her tummy. "Huh," she said. "That actually hadn't even crossed my mind." And, yay! The attention would be all on her.

"So, where do we start?" she asked.

"How about some jumping jacks to get our heart rates up?" Anders suggested.

Oh. He's really going to make me work out?

"My heart rate's beating plenty fast," Adelaide admitted, a sexy, practiced grin lifting her full lips. "But you're the expert here." Adelaide started jumping, noticing that both brothers' eyes were fixated on her. This wasn't awkward at all. Her breasts bounced freely, the sports bra more for looks than support. They didn't seem to mind.

"If I have to get sweaty, so do you, right?" she asked, hands on hips, when she was done.

"What would you have us do?" Anders asked. "We're at your disposal."

"Drop and give me twenty," she said. Adelaide was a sucker for arms and abs.

"Knuckles or one handed?" Anders asked.

Adelaide swallowed. "One handed sounds kind of hot," she admitted.

Anders dropped and started pumping out one-handed push-ups, his lean arms flexing with each rep.

Holy mother of God! Adelaide loved the long, lean lines of Anders's body. He looked like a runner, or a baseball player, with that tight, round ass.

Anders popped up, a cocky grin spreading across his face. It didn't last long, though, when Ari quietly crossed the room and reached his hand out for Adelaide. "You never did tell us your name," he said.

She accepted his hand, sparks of *something* shot through her entire body, like a current. It simmered and settled in her nether region, making her grow hot all over. It was an entirely pleasant feeling she wanted to explore more of. "You can call me Raine," she said, her throat suddenly parched.

"Raine," Ari repeated. "To quench my thirst . . ." he said with a quiet knowing, as if he recognized her.

Uh-oh. If he did, he didn't give her away.

"Take a seat," Ari said as he dropped down into push-up position on his knuckles.

"Where?" Adelaide asked, confused.

"On my back," he answered, grinning up at her with heated hazel eyes.

She looked at his broad back, muscles forming all kinds of ridges and planes. She suddenly wished she could lie down on his back and lick every square inch of muscled flesh. Instead, she sat, worried she would break his back. She wasn't a big girl, but she'd been a gymnast and cheerleader, and had nice strong legs and a little round booty to show for it. She quite enjoyed the feeling of his back beneath her warm center as she straddled him, holding on for dear life. Sure enough, he gave her twenty. Then he gave her twenty more, never breaking pace. She was sure he could feel her flood of excitement all over his back.

"Show off," Anders said, grinning.

"You're just jealous," Ari retorted, good naturedly.

"Not yet," Anders said, not so amused this time. "But I'm not so sure how I'll feel in two hours."

"Get over it," Ari said.

Anders lifted Adelaide off Ari's back and she suddenly missed the girth of his muscled back beneath her legs. Oh, what she wouldn't do to have him turn over so she could ride him another way.

Anders took Adelaide's hand and spun her into an embrace, so they were almost nose to nose. She was pressed up against his bare chest, void of any hair. He was so damn hot. *Almost too perfect.* "Ever work out on exercise balls before?" he asked, a mischievous look in his eyes.

"Sure," she said, looking around. "I don't see any though."

Ari started walking toward the bedroom. "Follow me," he instructed.

Adelaide watched as he entered the bedroom, his gorgeous backside disappearing behind the tall white doors. Her heart hammered when Anders leaned in closer, breathing gently on her ear with parted lips. "This is going to be the best workout of your life," he said, gently suckling her lobe. She melted against him, her hands holding onto his chest for support.

Anders ran his hand over her back, grabbing her ass as he bent down and brought his mouth to hers. His lips were warm, far softer than she would've imagined them to be. He looked all Scandinavian hot with a hard jawline and precise nose. But his lips . . . they were soft. His tongue, however . . .

He was definitely the alpha in this kiss. He took charge like he meant it, taking Adelaide's breathe away. "We may be sharing you, but you're mine in this room. We agreed to be respectful of each other and of you. But I'm staking my claim. You can explore one another, but only I'm going to bury myself deep inside you," he growled.

Adelaide's heat went into overdrive, a confused swirl of *hell no!* and *yes, sir!*

But, she had to admit, it was hot the way he took command. She reached down, cupping him over the workout pants he was wearing. He was rock hard already. Adelaide gently ran her hand up and down the length of him, her center aching.

"And what if I choose Ari instead," she taunted. She had no real objection to being fucked by Anders, as long as she had Ari in other ways. But she wasn't too keen on being told what to do.

A storm clouded Anders's blue eyes. He reached down and cupped her hot center, pressing his fingers up while rubbing back and forth. Though her booty shorts blocked him, the effect was the same. Adelaide's legs turned to Jell-O, and she instinctively leaned in toward his mouth. "Trust me," he whispered. "When I'm through with you, you will beg to have me be the one between your legs."

Christ!

His mouth took hers again, this time more demanding as he tugged at her ponytail with one hand and held her chin in the other. He'd moved her face perfectly for total domination. And she found it hot as hell.

When he was done, he stood back and their eyes locked. An understanding passed between them. Taking her hand in his, they walked to the bedroom. Inside there were three large white and silver exercise balls of various sizes. She had no idea what they were going to do with those, but she was intrigued.

The first thing she noticed when she entered the room was Ari, who stood before her completely naked, holding one of the exercise balls in his hands, strategically placed. *Dear God! That V though.*

If his arms had been impressive, his eight pack was even more so. Leading down to a delightful V pointing right to the goods. She couldn't wait to have him move the exercise ball so she could get the full picture. His hips were strong, and she suddenly felt an absence of him between her legs. Those hips were made for pumping. Whose idea had that been anyway? *Who needed honor?* huffed Adelaide to herself. The White Room was for abandoning inhibitions and taking risks. If she wanted them both, she would have them.

Satisfied, she walked toward Ari, lifting the gray hoodie over her head and tossing it to the floor. She knew he would be able to see right through the white bra top. It was tight and practically see through. Her nipples were high and perky, thanks to the reconstructive surgery she'd had after her preventative double mastectomy. She had scars, for sure. But her tits were beautiful and she was proud of them. Proud to be alive.

"So, Ari," Adelaide said huskily, "How are you planning to work me first?"

Ari's heated eyes raked over her chest, obvious lust kicking him in the gut as he appreciated her firm, round breasts. "Our workout today will be entirely on exercise balls. But first, we need to stretch you out."

She was standing directly on the other side of the inflated ball—the only thing standing in the way between her and Ari.

"Stretch me, then," she invited.

Ari dropped the ball and moved in. He lifted her arms over her head and spun her around fast so her back was pressed against the closest wall. Pure heat transcended Ari as his mouth found hers, her arms still pinned above her head in his firm grasp. She was panting, pressing her chest up against him, so wet just from that one kiss.

He leaned down, licking her neck and nibbling her clavicle. That's when she felt another set of hands lowering her booty shorts. *Oh my!* They weren't wasting any time.

Ari turned Adelaide around and leaned back against the wall himself, settling her against his chest and leaving her wide open to Anders. He lifted her sports bra over her head so she was completely naked and exposed.

Anders leaned forward while Ari pushed her long ponytail to the side and sucked the soft, delicate flesh of her neck. It was almost too much.

Even with her eyes closed, Adelaide could feel Anders trace his fingers over her scars, noticing them, but not spending all his time there. He touched her breasts; they were just a little bigger than his large palms and fit nicely as he massaged them. She felt the cool breeze from his breath on her nipple before she felt his warm tongue encase it, sucking greedily. She suspected he would be a hungry lover, and he didn't disappoint.

The sensations were too heady, too . . . complete. She felt full and safe in a way she never knew she could with two men. One cradling her back, one worshipping her front. She could feel Ari's length pressing against her, rock hard but patient. She reached back and stroked him slowly, enjoying the soft feel of skin as Anders' tongue explored lower, lower until hot lips circled her clit. She moaned, loving the way his tongue danced over her folds, the pace of her hand stroking Ari mirroring the exact tempo.

A dance she never wanted to end.

Fingers dove deep as Anders stood, pressing them far inside as he came up for a kiss. Possessive. Adelaide reached out and nipped his lip, sucking it in and running her tongue over it. She was ready for something else in her mouth, but would go at their pace.

Anders took her hand, leading her over to one of the exercise balls. "Here, sit on this one so your back is flat against it. I'll support your weight at the legs."

Adelaide did as she was told, feeling the cool rubber against her back as she lay flat. The ball gave, rolling gently beneath her, but Anders quickly steadied her legs, putting them over his shoulders. When she looked up, she saw he was sitting flat on the floor, the ball between his legs. He steadied her with his hands as they reached around her thighs, his head diving between her legs as he worked her with his tongue.

Oh, God!

The man knew his way around. He was fierce, latching on and

not relenting. Her hips bucked, but he kept sucking her sensitive nub. Somewhere above hands massaged her breasts again, but this time they were bigger, rougher. *Ari.*

He pinched her nipples, gently pulling each one up. She no longer had the sensation she once had, but the tugging itself seared her to the core. Rough calluses scraped her neck as he guided her head, her mouth, to open for him. He leaned over her from behind and kissed her upside down. It was the single sexiest kiss she'd ever had. Images of Spider-Man kissing Mary Jane in the rain washed over her. Ari couldn't possibly know it, but that's why she chose the name Raine for the White Room. Her insides ached, longing coursing through her.

His tongue was wider than Anders'—thick, warm, and sensuous. It was the tongue of a man's man. He licked the outside of her bottom lip, playfully nipping at it. She reached her hands up, cradling the sides of his face as he did. While Anders's tongue was keeping her body busy, it was Ari's tongue that would keep her up at night. If a kiss could ever feel better than making love—this was the one.

Adelaide sucked in his tongue, bathing it. She ran her fingers in Ari's hair as he gently rolled her breasts in his hands.

He pulled back, breaking the kiss, and whispered in her ear, "Will you take me?"

Based on her conversation with Anders earlier, she was sure Ari meant with her mouth. She nodded, eager to taste him.

Anders slid three fingers deep inside her just as she reached up and invited Ari's cock inside her mouth. She'd never sucked a man like this before, upside down, but she found it an easy angle, enjoyed the feel of his hands on her head as he guided himself in her mouth while steadying her on the ball. He was so big she couldn't take him all the way down. But she reached up and worked his shaft with her hands while she took what she could in her throat. She'd give just about anything to feel that wide cock of his slide deep inside of her. But it was Anders who slid in now.

She couldn't help but cry out when he thrust himself in deep, taking her by surprise by the length of him. Ari backed away, leaving her missing the feel of him. But she was soon distracted. Anders was standing, his legs bent as he held her hips up to his waist. He drove deep inside her, again and again, the ball giving under their weight as he bottomed her out. Adelaide whimpered as she came, fireworks exploding behind closed eyes. Her body shook, ripples of pleasure washing over her. Slowly, he eased her legs down, her body still trembling with delicious afterquakes.

Without pulling out, he lifted her off the ball, his arms cradling her back as he leaned in for a kiss. The feel of his strong arms wrapped around her back, his mouth soft and warm after such an intense orgasm, soothed her. Helped her breath come back to normal.

Anders pulled out, lifting Adelaide off of the ball. He led her over to the largest ball, one that would support his weight. "I want you to ride me, Raine," he said. The sound of her name startled her after thinking of it being tied to Ari just moments ago. She looked up and met Ari's eyes. She couldn't read his full expression, but lust still lingered there, heated and strong. She wanted to please him, make him feel as good as her body hummed right now.

Adelaide cocked a finger in his direction and called him to come hither with the sexiest bedroom eyes she had. Ari wasted no time crossing the room, taking her in his arms. He consumed her. There was no other word for it. Anders may have wanted to possess her, but Ari *did* possess her. Every cell shook in recognition as he reached one hand up behind her head and wrapped the other one around her waist, pulling her in with force as he drowned her in kisses. Adelaide's body was a puddle fusing against his; she could hardly tell where his body started and hers ended. Her hands flew everywhere, tracing the muscles of his back, grasping his hips. She wanted to drag him to the bed and have her dirty way with him.

Adelaide knew from Arianna that the rules had changed, that clients could see past lovers if the feeling was mutual. She knew without a doubt she would request him again; she wouldn't feel fully satisfied until she'd felt him slide inside her, too. She couldn't leave that question unanswered if just a kiss elicited this reaction.

When they parted she was breathless, her chest rising and falling in time to her erratic heart. They stood apart, their eyes never wavering. Gold. He had flecks of gold in them. They went gray when they were stormy. Golden when they—when they what? She wasn't quite sure what he was feeling.

But she felt the absence of him, even as Anders guided her hips down onto his cock. He was lying on his back on the new exercise ball, his shaft strong and ready for her. Her desire was so deep right now she didn't care where the release came from. She needed another orgasm to scratch the unfettered desire that raged deep inside.

Her back was to Anders as she rode him, her hips rolling with the length of him buried deep inside. She had to look away from Ari for just a moment as she sighed, loving the feel of him hitting her so deeply. She eased forward so he could hit her G-spot. Rocking back and forth, she took and released. He held onto her hips to steady himself, but it was Adelaide who was doing the fucking.

She reached down and rubbed her clit, her insides tingling from the heightened sensitivity. When she opened her eyes, she saw Ari was watching her, stroking himself as she pleasured herself. She had no idea what he thought as she fucked Anders, but his eyes never left hers, as if they were the only two in the room.

But they weren't, and Adelaide quite enjoyed the long, strong length and athleticism Anders offered. He was a fucking machine. She sat upright, rubbing her breasts in her own hands and inviting Ari over with her eyes. Now it was Anders who was in control as he thrust his hips up and pulled back down, making her feel every slow inch of him as he moved in and out.

He slowed his pace so Adelaide could take Ari in her mouth

again, and she appreciated that. She wrapped both hands around Ari's cock, twisting back and forth as her mouth slid over him, getting him wet to help her hands slide better. Her tongue circled him, over and over, like a giant ice pop. She lapped up one side and down the other, darting her tongue over his sac as she rubbed him. He held onto her head, slowly moving his hips back and forth as he fucked her mouth. Instinctively, her hands reached around to cup his ass, her hands getting a rock-hard handful of steel buns.

She loved the way it felt as he flexed each time he pumped forward, inviting her to taste him. He leaned over and whispered in her ear, brushing his mouth over it and sending shivers coursing throughout her entire body.

"Can I come in your mouth?" he asked. She'd never really had anyone ask that before. Adelaide's guess was that they assumed it was okay. And it was, or she wouldn't have let them. But still.

She nodded her head, tearing away to meet his lips. His hands cupped her face again, his tongue dominating hers. Somewhere in the background she felt the tip of Anders's cock reach her deepest crevices again, and she moaned into Ari's mouth.

The sensation of two completely different lovers and two completely different styles of making love was indescribable. She felt a little lost, out of control. Images of them both fucking her at the same time flashed before her eyes. She wanted them everywhere.

Anders reached up, arching behind her and grasping her breasts as he held her all the way down on his cock. As she took Ari in her mouth and began sucking again, Anders pumped. He used the leverage of the ball to pull back and slam inside her. She moaned even as her tongue worshipped Ari's girth. Her hands worked his shaft just as fast as the pace Anders was setting as he plunged in and out. She grew lightheaded, the sensation overwhelming all of her senses.

Then Ari gripped her head again, thrust his pelvis one last time, and shook, his body spasming as he released inside of her mouth. She sucked hard, drawing him in, using her tongue to lick the remains. He was absolutely gorgeous, his body sweaty and ripped as he looked down at her, ran his fingers through her hair. He leaned over, taking her mouth in his own as he kissed her.

She gasped, shocked that he was kissing her so intimately, so completely, right after. But she leaned in, took his tongue and worshipped it as she just had something else. It was Ari's gentle grasp of her face as he kissed her that ignited the warm flames in her belly; but it was Anders who brought her home, burning down the whole damn house. She felt him thrust as far as he could inside her and knew he was going to come. His fingers grasped both sides of her hips as he called out, "God, come with me, Raine."

And she did. She released again, her body shuddering, rocking back and forth as she came. Coming down, down, down from euphoria somewhere. Uncertain where her heart, mind, and body had just ventured.

Anders's guttural growl from deep within brought her back to reality. She was being held firm down on his stomach as he arched into her, exploding.

Her insides warmed, filling her tummy with heat. She was on the pill, and they were tested, so she wasn't concerned. But she'd never had two men explode inside of her like that before. She wished she could share the experience with Arianna, have someone to process it with, but she couldn't; not when she couldn't wrap her own head around it.

She started to giggle, her body shaking as she rose off of Anders to a full stand. When her body went limp from all of the exertion, it was Ari who caught her. He held her to his chest, letting her drop her head and catch her breath before trying to walk. She could hear his heart beating, enjoyed the gentle bump-bump, bump-bump. She heard that when your hearts synced, you were connected.

Anders came up behind her, rubbing her shoulders and kissing her neck. He was enveloping her from behind, kissing her sensually as she listened to the pitter-patter of Ari's heart. She leaned her head back, opening her neck to Anders. While her back was pressed up against him, her chest was still touching Ari's.

Somewhere in the distance she heard the bell chime. But she was lost in a dreamland of soft kisses on the front of her throat and the back of her neck. She never wanted her time there to end.

It was then that she realized their hearts were in sync. Not just hers and Ari's . . . but hers and Anders', as well.

CHAPTER 13
AVALINE

Avaline's nerves were shot. She'd had about three hours of sleep and cursed this morning when she realized she was out of her miracle under-eye cream. Of all days. Still, she walked over to the nearly twenty-foot-tall mirror and smoothed her hands over her Bordeaux-colored lace dress. The neck was high, but the lace had no lining around her chest and down the long sleeves. Classy, but sexy—Avaline's go-to style of choice.

Although she'd just come from a friend's wedding, she'd been looking forward to this evening for over a year and wanted to look her best.

She was finally going to see him again.

Butterflies took flight in her tummy as the double doors opened. Her mouth ran dry when she saw him stroll in, black on black tuxedo and just as sexy as she remembered him.

He stopped cold when he lifted those sexy, whiskey-colored eyes and met hers.

Does he even recognize me?

He crossed the room in three long strides and took her face in both hands, crushing his mouth down on hers. She was drowning in him. His tongue, his taste, his scent . . . exactly how she remembered, even after all these months.

When he pulled back, she felt void of air, of life itself. He rested his forehead on hers, meeting her eyes. "Emmeline," he rasped, "why haven't you agreed to see me before now?"

Pain. So much pain in his voice.

She gazed deeply into his vibrant brown eyes, wanting to stay lost in them forever. How could she tell him? Would he even understand?

Dom had requested her every single week for the past six months, ever since the board voted unanimously to change the rules and allow clients to repeat visits with favorite lovers. Hell, he hadn't even been back to the White Room in well over a year, not since their last encounter, to be precise.

"Dom . . ." She took his hand and walked him into the living room, where she'd had a fire started for them. A beautiful white faux bearskin rug covered the white carpet beneath. She was praying they would make good use of it later. "There's so much to explain. Can I get you a drink first?"

"Whiskey, straight," was all he said, his hands in his pockets, his dress shirt unbuttoned with the tuxedo tie hanging loose.

Dear God. He was everything Avaline remembered and more. He was slightly trimmer now. Leaner. But he filled out every inch of that tuxedo like a man born to wear one. She walked over to the hidden bar, opening the mirrored doors. She neatly poured two whiskeys and carried them over to Dom.

"Here, sit with me by the fire, won't you?" she asked. She'd had a special love seat brought in for this occasion. It forced them to sit closer while they talked. And she needed to talk to him before they could go any further. Needed to know where his heart was, and not just his penis. Had she been more to him? Or just a residual itch from a one-night stand that he needed to scratch again?

Because he'd been so much more than that to Avaline. He was the reason she changed the rules. The reason she'd gone on after Henri's death.

She swallowed, fidgeting with her hands, which were nestled in her lap. Dom joined her on the tall love seat, taking his whiskey from her as he sat. He stared at her over the rim as he sipped, letting the warm liquid burn its way down. But he said nothing.

"Dom, I don't even know where to start. You've crossed my mind so many times over the past year—"

She drew in a lungful of air, shaky.

"Then why haven't you requested me once after the rules changed?" he asked, turning away and staring off into the flames. "Damn it! I couldn't believe my luck when I heard that they'd changed the rules," he said, dragging his hand over his nearly bald head.

"Emmeline—you haven't just crossed my mind over the past year. You've fucking lived there."

Avaline's heart constricted as if everything in her world was tilting into place, making sense for the first time in years.

"Not only have you lived there, you've taken up permanent residence. Shared my bed. Had coffee with me on my patio. Every waking minute I had the image of those gorgeous hazel eyes searing into my memory. The way you parted your lips, the feel of your hair."

He reached up, running his fingers through her soft waves. "It's exactly as soft as I remember," he said hoarsely.

"Dom—stop." Avaline stood, taking a healthy sip of her whiskey. It burned so good going down. She was usually a white wine kind of woman, but this whiskey was exactly like Dom—strong, solid, hot as fuck.

He grabbed her hand and stood, facing her. "I can't, Emmeline—"

"My real name is Avaline Bellarose," she whispered. "It's time you knew the truth."

He paused, searching her face. "Avaline, huh?" A grin lifted the corner of his mouth, a predatory look crossing his dark eyes. They grew darker when he was aroused; she remembered that from before. They were like black pools of lust at the moment.

"Yes. I'm sorry I didn't tell you the first time, but . . . rules."

"Fuck the rules, Avaline. It's the goddamn rules that kept me from you this past year." He wrapped one arm around her waist, the other holding the back of her head as he drew her against his body, pressing her so they were chest to chest. Goddamn, she was a handful of liquid heat. White heat. The kind that glowed so bright it seared your soul.

She stood on her toes, bringing her lips softly to his. Her hands covered the top of his head, rubbing it as their tongues reunited, slowly this time, remembering. She never wanted to stop kissing him, but they had to talk first, she was determined—though he wasn't making it easy. His hands wrapped around her waist, cupping her ass to draw her in even closer. She felt him then. So wide and hard beneath the pants of his tuxedo.

"God, Dom . . . wait. I want to explain something first, okay? I—I can't think when you're this close." She stood back, her chest heaving. She ran her tongue over her lips, tasting him there.

"Thinking's overrated, Avaline. I haven't touched you in more than a year. You are all I've thought about. Can you at least tell me you felt the same?"

She lowered her head, nodding. But when she lifted her eyes they were wet, tears forming behind her long, black lashes. Dom rushed in, pulling her close. He ran his hand over the back of her head, nestling it to his chest protectively. "Shit, Avaline. Please don't cry. What's wrong?"

He held her there, letting her catch her breath. Then he led her back to the love seat, sat next to her, and took her hands in his. She swallowed, knowing there was only one way to get through to the future she wanted. She had to brave the fire.

"I have thought about you so many times, Dom. But you know I was married. I told you that when we met."

Dom pursed his lips together, looking away.

"There's so much more, Dom. It gets worse before it gets better."

"What could be worse than you having a husband, Avaline?" he growled, his eyes growing misty too.

"Him dying," she whispered.

"Fuck," Dom said, dragging her into his lap. He held her while she cried, her head resting on his shoulder. He cradled her, stroking her hair. Giving her the time she needed to collect herself. She turned to face him. They were close. So close.

"I loved Henri, you have to know that. He was much older than I was, but I loved him. His children had a hard time believing that when we first married—thought I was after his money." She laughed dryly. "I never needed his money. I needed him."

"Avaline, I'm so sorry," Dom said, holding her hands and tracing her skin with the pad of his thumb.

"Thank you. It's just important for me to be honest with you."

"Why?" he asked quietly. "You don't owe me anything. I was no one to you," he said, pulling back.

"That's not true, Dom. And I think you know that," she whispered. "You were what got me through the toughest days of my life. You were the strength I needed when I watched him deteriorate. The idea that I could see you again, seek refuge in your arms—*that* was enough to make me go on. You, Dom. You were worth fighting for."

He couldn't wait. He had to have her. To love her. To ease the sorrow from her eyes. Their kiss started slowly at first, till he bit her lower bit, drawing it in. Her hands flew everywhere—hungry. Starving for his skin.

He reached around, unzipped the back of her dress as he kissed her neck, taking solace under her chin. He buried his face in her hair, kissing along her forehead and down her nose. Slid her dress off her shoulders.

She stood, letting it fall the rest of the way to the ground and revealing the long legs he remembered. The creamy white skin. Like last time, she favored black lace under her dress, her bra pushing up in all the right ways to form two perfect globes. He reached out, stroking his fingers along the tops of her breasts, dipping his finger between the valley. She sighed, dropping her head back, opening herself to him.

He went slow, cupping her breasts as he kissed the tops of them. With one quick movement, he unsnapped her bra, revealing the most flawless breasts he'd ever seen. Petite, pink nipples stared back at him, begging for his tongue to worship them. He'd worship at her altar for the rest of his life if she'd let him.

He flicked his tongue over the sensitive nub that called to him. Her breasts were high and round. But soft. So freaking soft. He took her entire areola in his mouth, sucking hard, bringing a rush of blood to the surface and coloring her porcelain flesh. Love bites. She'd have marks in the morning, and he was glad. He wanted her to remember him. Wanted to leave a trail of evidence of their lovemaking so she would never forget him again.

"Dom—" she said.

"We'll talk later. I've waited a year to hold you in my arms again, Avaline. You're mine now," he said, crushing her lips with his own. "At least for tonight, let me have you—let me love you."

It was all she needed. Her hands flew, removing his tuxedo jacket and tie in record time. Buttons snapped in haste as she worked her way to his perfectly sculpted chest. Just as she remembered. Except now, he had the tattoo of a moonflower on his chest, right over his heart. She'd recognize the shape anywhere. It's white-pink blossoms looked like a full moon and only bloomed at night—kind of like their last time together. Sacred, magical . . . gone in the morning.

She slowed, tracing her fingers over the delicate, pointed petals twisting together to form a near circle. Just as they did in her garden. "How?" she asked.

Dom leaned in, inhaling the scent from her skin before bringing his lips to hers in a soft, slow-simmering kiss. "You smelled like night flowers the first time I met you," he admitted. "And you had them in the room. Every time I see one, I think of you. Remember the scent of you all over me. So"—he pointed to his chest—"I got one tattooed on my skin. Over my heart. Because I'll always think of you and remember how rare they are, how rare you are, when I see it. And you have my heart, Avaline. You've had it since the first time you walked through those damn doors."

She cried out, unable to catch her breath. "It was only one time. I'm sure you've had other lovers since then."

"Once was enough, Avaline—when it was with you. There has never been another woman as classy and sexy as you in my life. That spark that happened when we first met—it felt . . ." he searched for words. "I'm not good at this Avaline. I'm a fighter—*was* a fighter. Not a poet."

His grin was feral, full of heat. "But it felt intoxicatingly familiar and brand new all at once."

He lifted her chin with his hand, turning her face up to his. "I know you're still grieving, and I promise to give you all the space you need. But I need you, Avaline. Let me make love to you—just for tonight."

Tears pooled in her eyes, dripping down her cheeks. He leaned forward, kissed them from her skin, then took her mouth in his. "Let me love away your pain, Avaline."

She nodded, slowly unbuttoning his tuxedo pants. He was always commando underneath—old habits died hard. She placed her hands on his chest, bent forward to kiss him, tongue meeting skin as she savored. Remembering his scent, his taste. Everything about their first night flooded back to her.

Pushing him up against the conference room table and freeing him. Tasting him. Trusting him. Letting him blindfold her. Spread her wide open on the table so he could devour her.

Her whole body shivered. She'd had lovers since Dom, but not over the last six months. Not while sitting day by day at Henri's side. And not since she lost him.

She was hungry for Dom. Ravenous.

She shimmied his pants down his legs, dropping to her knees so she could help him step out of them. Avaline removed his dress shoes and socks, one at a time, before leaving a trail of kisses up his strong legs. She knew he was a fighter—had been? She wanted to hear more, but there were more pressing things to attend to first.

His skin was warm, manly. His legs hairy and strong. She ran her hands up the back of his thighs as she kissed his quads, her tongue loving a path along his inner thigh. His body twitched as Dom's hands dropped to her hair. He lifted it to a ponytail so he could see her face.

She looked up at him, her hazel eyes bewitching his heart

further. One lick and he was a goner. His head dropped back as her tongue ran the length of him. Her hot mouth covered him, taking him down, down, down. Her small hands cupped him below, rolling his sac between her fingers as she sucked on him. Dom wanted to touch her, have his fingers inside her at the same time.

"Get up," he growled. He tugged her hair, loved meeting her eyes over his cock.

Avaline stood, following him to the love seat. He helped her recline, her back pressed against one of the tall armrests while he stood next to her. He placed a foot on the sofa as she guided his cock back into her mouth, moaning as he touched her breasts and teased her sensitive nipples.

He let one of his hands wander south until he found her sleek, warm center. He pushed her black lace thong aside, appreciating the small triangle of her hair. Dom circled her sensitive nub with his thumb, rubbing his fingers along her outer folds. As her pace quickened with her mouth, he moved his hand, sliding three fingers deep inside her. She was so wet and it felt so familiar, even after all this time. She wrapped around his fingers perfectly, as if she were made just for him.

He matched the pace she set, driving deep, bending his fingers so he could reach her G-spot. Avaline lifted her hips, her body rolling like a line of waves as she arched into his hand over and over again. He couldn't take it any longer. "You need to stop, Avaline, or I'm going to come," he warned. She used her hands to pull his ass closer, refusing to let go.

Fuck!

He drove his fingers in deeper, faster. She met his hand thrust for thrust as if it were his cock. But her mouth stayed latched, persistent. He gave in, goose bumps washing over him as a primal groan escaped his lips. He came, deep inside her throat. He couldn't take his eyes off her as she licked her way back to the top, his fingers never ceasing their pace. His body was still twitching with little aftershocks when she called out his name.

"Oh, God, Dom. Yes! I'm so close." Her hands went to her nipples, squeezing them as his fingers danced, his thumb closing over her clit. Now that he was free, he bent down, bridging the gap between her hot opening and his mouth. He sucked in, tugged at her flesh. She cried out again, clutching his ears as he buried his face in deep, grinding his mouth back and forth on her and not letting go.

She bucked her body in blissed-out agony, on the brink of orgasm. Dom didn't know what came over him, but he grabbed both of her legs and flipped them over her head, her knees by her ears, so he could draw her pussy up even closer to his mouth. He held onto her hips as he devoured her, lashing her warm center with his tongue. It was so primal, so instinctual, so fucking boss—she came instantly, a long, intense orgasm as he held onto her clit, not letting her loose until she rode the wave of pleasure all the way down.

Her hands fell above her head, laughter escaping her lips. "Oh. My. God. Dom."

"I know, right?" he said, a cocky grin on his wet lips. He took her hand and helped her sit up.

"That was even better than I remembered," she admitted.

Dom ran his hand across his mouth, the scent of her all over his face. He never wanted to wash it off. But he wanted to make love to her on that sexy-ass bearskin rug, so he grabbed her hand and led her to the bathroom.

The floor was heated to just the right temperature. He loved watching her walk in front of him. She still had on her thong, and the back rode high above her butt cheeks, giving him the sexiest show. Her high heels click-clacked across the tile floor until she reached the shower. Avaline leaned over to remove her wet thong and unfasten the straps of her black heels. She met his eyes as she stood, tossing the shoes to the side with a flick of her ankles. The look she gave him as she stepped into the shower could have melted icecaps.

He didn't waste any time joining her. They stood under the hot spray, holding onto one another for the longest time. It was as if they were afraid to let go. His arms circled her, letting her rest her head against his chest. She'd been through so much this past year, and he wanted nothing more than to protect her. Know everything about her and what she'd been through. Then love the rest of the pain away.

He dropped his head, kissing the top of her hair, brushing it over her shoulder. If at all possible, she was even sexier wet. Her long dark brown hair dripped down her back like a river running wild. He remembered taking her from behind on the conference room table; she had a small waist, but a nice, round, heart-shaped ass he so badly wanted to spank again.

He pressed her up against the glass of the shower, leaning in to take her full, soft lips in his own. Her cranberry lipstick had long since disappeared on his cock. She stood on her toes to meet his mouth, her tongue taking the lead while her hands ran over his short brush cut. She moaned, pressing against him. The scent of lemon and rosemary filled the steamed-up shower as he lathered her body. Suds ran down her perky breasts, over her taut stomach, and between her legs. She slid up and down against him as they kissed, driving him to the brink of distraction.

He could take no more.

He turned her hot little body around and rubbed his hands up and down her bubbled-up sides, cupping her breasts. She pushed her ass against the hard-on that was riding tall up against her backside. She wiggled her body as Dom stroked it, sliding her butt cheeks up and down the length of him, sudsing him up in the process.

Her tits were the perfect size, his hands slipping and sliding easily over them with all the bubbles. She arched back and kissed him slowly as he pinched her nipples hard, tugging them. When they came up for air, he placed a hand on her back and guided her forward so he could slide inside her warm, wet opening.

Memories flooded him of their first time together. She was just as tight and hot as he remembered, but this time was even better. This time, she was free.

He buried himself deep inside, grinding his hips against her ass as he rocked back and forth. Her palms pressed against the slick tile as he filled her, lightning shooting to her stomach when he grabbed her long, thick hair and tugged. Her scalp tingled, her insides aching even as he filled her.

Avaline met him thrust for thrust, sliding even farther down his long shaft as he rubbed the bubbles over the slick, perfect globes of her ass. Her insides clenched around his cock in pleasure when he slipped his wet thumb into her backside, sliding it back and forth as he drove into her, his pace never slowing. Her body spasmed against him, her legs shaking as she came again. He nearly exploded with her, but he wanted so much more.

When she'd come down from her orgasm and her breathing evened, he turned her around to face him, kissing the tip of her nose. "Wow," she breathed out, her teeth finding his lower lip and tugging, sucking it in. She wrapped her hands around his waist, gripping his ass.

"We're not done yet," he growled. The heat was boiling in his stomach, and only she could put out this fire.

They rinsed off and stepped out of the shower. As he was drying her off with a large, white, fluffy towel, he heard the chime go off and cursed. "No! It's not enough time, damn it."

"Shh," she said, pressing a finger over his mouth. "We have more time," she promised.

He kissed her finger. "How?"

"Come, follow me, and I'll tell you the rest of my story," she said.

They bundled up in plush white robes, emblazoned with WR on the left breast pocket. They headed back to the living room, to their cocoon by the fire. There was a fresh tray with hot chocolate waiting for them, just as she'd ordered from the concierge. White moonflowers filled the vase on the tray.

Dom grinned, fingering the petals. "Would you like some?" he asked.

She nodded, sitting on the bearskin rug and looking into the fire. There were monstrous piles of white pillows surrounding them on the floor. He carried two mugs over and sat beside her, handing her one.

She cupped the warm mug with both hands, getting lost in the flames that danced before her. She felt his hand on her back, rubbing his palm in circles but giving her the silent space she needed.

"Okay," she said, taking a deep breath. "Ready for the rest of it?"

Dom nodded, taking a sip.

"My husband Henri and I own the White Room," she said, pausing to gauge his reaction.

She understood the confusion she saw fill his eyes. "All this time? You've owned it?" Dom ran a hand over his face. Avaline knew the wheels were spinning in his head, and she braced herself for the question she knew was coming. "You could have called me. If it's your company, you could have seen me anytime you wanted to."

"I was still married, Dom. The rules we created were meant to protect our clients. No matter how I felt personally, our time together *had* to be compartmentalized and kept in the White Room. I couldn't live with myself otherwise."

"Of course. I know, Avaline. I just—it's a lot to wrap my head around, and I missed you so fucking much." Dom held her hands in his own, squeezing them. "I'm sorry . . . go on."

Avaline nodded, rubbing her thumb over his fingers. "As soon as we found out he was sick—he had Creutzfeldt-Jakob's disease, the hereditary kind—we transferred the entire company over to me. Have you ever heard of that disease before?" Avaline asked.

"No," Dom said shaking his head. "You said it was hereditary? Did you have children together?"

"No," she whispered. "We never did. We thought we had all the time in the world. Turns out we didn't." Avaline frowned, closing her eyes for a moment. When she opened them, her gaze settled on the fire that crackled before them, a welcome distraction. "He has kids from his first marriage though."

"I'm sorry to hear that, Avaline. It must have been a terrible year for you. I'm sorry I ever mentioned you not reaching out to me or accepting my invitations back to this room. That was selfish of me."

She shook her head. "You didn't know. You couldn't have. My husband wanted me happy, though. His body and mind began deteriorating quickly after we found out about his condition. When we first married, I knew he was the CEO of the White Room, but I never used it. I never needed to. But after he was diagnosed, and his health started to decline, my life revolved completely around his care and learning how to run the business; he insisted I give myself this time. To be a woman. To forget about the ugly business of going from wife to caregiver. To experience a different reality, I suppose, than the one I was living."

Avaline toyed with the soft fur beneath her fingers. "I never wanted to, at first. But then I realized how badly I needed the touch, the connections. We stopped going to church. We could no longer host parties. Our life together became about making our last memories together. Because soon, he lost those too."

Avaline cried silent tears, using the lapel of her robe to wipe them. Dom wrapped his arms around her and lifted her chin. "We don't have to talk about this if you're not ready," he said.

"I'm ready. I need you to know so we can start with a clean slate. I don't want any secrets between us."

Dom felt hopeful for the first time in years. *So we can start with a clean slate.* That implied they would see each other again.

"So, you own and run this entire company now?" Dom asked,

intimidated but not wanting to show his cards.

"Well, not the entire company. The Wells family cofounded the White Room with my husband and still owns forty percent. I have a managing board for major decisions. And over the last year, I've been slowly delegating the day-to-day responsibilities by hiring new directors for all the major divisions we have. More goes into the White Room than you'd imagine."

"And *you* changed the rules?"

Avaline blushed. "I did."

"Why, Avaline?" He ran his hand up her neck and behind her head. "I need to hear why you did."

He scorched her with the heated look in his eyes, and she suspected he'd already connected the dots.

"I changed the rules because of you," she said, low and heated. "I'd never met anyone like you before—in or out of the White Room. There was just *something* there I couldn't forget. When I was sad or lonely, I thought of you. When something happened and I wanted to celebrate, I wished I could call you."

"You could have though," he said, studying her. "If you own the company, you have access to my files, right?"

"Yes and no," she said. "I can pull parts of them up, but we keep a lot of the data encoded for safety. But I read your basic profile, yes," she admitted.

"So you know I haven't been back, right?" he said huskily.

Avaline nodded, biting her lip.

"You are all I fucking thought about, Avaline. From the moment we touched, there was something undeniable about our connection. Something I couldn't ignore. Tell me you felt it too," he said, searching her eyes.

"It's why I changed the rules, Dom. I needed to see you again. I had your file, but it's encrypted. The contact information is only accessible by computer, but isn't visible in any records. First names only, last names encrypted."

"Burrows," he said. "It's Dominick Michael Burrows."

"Burrows," she whispered, a flash of recognition lighting her eyes. "Oh my God. My husband used to watch you on TV. You're an MMA fighter, right?"

"A champion," he said. "Until I quit."

"What?" Avaline looked up, searching his eyes. "Why did you quit fighting if you were so successful?"

"It's a dangerous job, Avaline. One wrong punch to the head and I'm out of a job . . . or worse."

"But that's a risk you took every time you got into a ring, right?"

"It was," he said, nodding.

"So what made you give it up? It must have been an exciting career," she said.

"You."

"Me?" Avaline furrowed her brow, running her hand along the

top part of his furry leg that was peeking out of the bathrobe.

"I'm not a rule follower, Avaline. I knew sooner or later I'd get in touch with you. I knew you were married, so I didn't exactly have a plan. But I needed to see you again. When I found out they changed the rules—*you* changed the rules—I wanted out. I didn't want to get hurt in the ring. I didn't want to get so badly fucked up I could never see you again. So I cashed in my career, opened a business, and now I train new up and-coming fighters."

Avaline didn't know what to say. He'd given up a career he loved after one night together. She didn't know whether to be concerned or turned on. It was definitely the later. "You did that, for me?"

Dom shrugged. "Mostly," he said. "I—I also found out I was a father."

"After we were together?" Avaline asked. She had no right. She'd been with several other lovers since Dom. She never even knew if she would see him again. He could've been with anyone he wanted.

"No. Needless to say, the earlier years in my career were a little more reckless. I came up in the circuit quickly, gaining a lot of notoriety the more fights I won."

"Yeah, Henri made a pretty penny off you a few times," Avaline admitted, laughing.

Dom grinned. "That's all right," he said admirably. "Well, about a month after our first time together here, I got a phone call. It was from a woman I'd met through my trainer at the start of my career —

his cousin or something like that. I can't remember the connection. She sort of tagged along off and on for a few months with us. Real free spirit. I didn't take her too seriously, but I didn't have my shit together back then either. Partied a little too hard after my wins. All that adrenaline doesn't go away on its own. It'll downright eat you alive if you don't get rid of it somehow. Others turned to drugs. Women were my outlet."

He looked up at Avaline, remorse filling his eyes. "I wish I could change things, Avaline, but I can't. Not about my daughter, but about my past. My daughter is the best thing that's ever happened to me."

A light filled Dom's eyes that brightened the more he talked about his daughter.

"What's her name?" Avaline asked.

"Dusty Rose. Kind of a hippy name if you ask me, but I didn't exactly get a say in the matter."

"So the mother never told you about her? How old is she?" Avaline asked.

"Five," he said, low. "Her mom suspected I was the father, but never came to me after she was pregnant. I remembered her, of course, but we weren't exactly a couple. She helped me forget about some stuff I'd rather not remember."

Avaline nodded, but didn't push. "So you're a daddy," she said, her eyes softening as she looked at Dom.

"Does that worry you?" The thought hadn't crossed his mind

until Avaline told him that she and her husband hadn't had children together. Maybe she had no interest in them, especially at this stage in her life.

"Not at all. I've always wanted kids of my own."

She moved toward him, straddling his lap. She could feel him hard and firm beneath her. She lifted the lapels of his robe and pulled him closer. "It's kind of sexy," she admitted. She bent her head, taking his lips in hers. Caressing them softly with her tongue. "As long as the mom's not in the picture," she growled into his ear.

Dom laughed. "She's nowhere in sight, other than to hand off Dusty Rose from time to time." He ran his hands up under her robe, along her outer thighs. "So, what now?" he asked, burying his face in her hair and kissing her neck.

"Right now, you slide inside me," she whispered.

He didn't have to be asked twice. He lifted Avaline and slid her down on top of his cock, always ready and hard for her. Dom sprinkled kisses over her shoulders as he ran his hands down her arms, removing the robe. She was more than he ever dreamed for himself. He didn't know what happened after right now, but right now, he was exactly where he wanted to be.

Avaline was straddling him, her knees landing on both sides of his body. Her hands went to his chest, pressing her bottom down so she could ride him. Their bodies moved in rhythm as if they were made to love each other this way.

When they came, they came together, unspoken but connected.

"Dom," she cried out, her body shaking as they collapsed, completely spent. Avaline snuggled into him, spooning into his side and placing her head in the crook of his arm. He rubbed her arm with his other hand, languishing there, taking his time.

"Avaline," he said, his voice raspy. "I know I have no right to ask this, especially after all you've been through. But please tell me there's an 'after this.' It doesn't have to be today; it doesn't have to be tomorrow—though I'm okay if it is," he said, laughing. "But I was so scared I'd never see you again. I can't walk away from you a second time."

Avaline studied the lines of his face. The scruff lining his jaw, his neck. Hooded brown eyes the color of the whiskey they'd shared bored into her, searching for answers she had spent the last six months trying to find for herself. She sat up on her elbow, her eyes never leaving his. The emotions that flooded through her were real. There was no confusion. No transference. These feelings were genuine and they were for Dom.

"This year has dragged me through hell and back, Dom. The life I knew before completely died. I'm still grieving, because I did love Henri. But I knew for a while that I was losing him, so I prepared my heart for the inevitable. Well, you can never really prepare for something like that, but I did the best I could.

"And then I met you. You weren't supposed to happen to me. I wasn't supposed to find love again. I thought I'd grow old and just have a string of lovers from the White Room," she said and smiled when Dom growled. "Now I know how empty and shallow that existence would have been. How unhappy it would have made me."

Dom pushed a strand of her hair behind her ear, ran his fingers along her face. "Did you just use the L word?" he asked, grinning.

Avaline swatted his chest playfully. "I think a small part of me started falling for you the moment I walked through those doors, Dom. I've never met a man who owns the space as much as you do. You were so confident, arrogant almost, in the way you made love to me that first day. Sure, it was hot. But it also spoke volumes about the type of man you are." Avaline blushed, lowering her head so her hair fell over his chest, covering her face.

He lifted her chin. "Look at me, Avaline," he commanded.

She peered up at him, with fresh eyes. Seeing the man who had fought so hard to get to her again. The man who wouldn't give up on her.

Dominick.

Henri had been the most beautiful part of her past. Her heart still had cracks she wasn't sure would ever fully heal. But when she looked at Dom, she saw something different. She saw her future.

"I *have* loved you since the moment I first saw you. I never believed in love at first sight—thought it was just an asshole line guys used to get in a girl's pants. But when you walked through those doors . . . talk about owning a space. You completely stripped the fucking air from my lungs, Avaline. I couldn't breathe.

"I've never been knocked on my ass so hard in my life. Nothing in the cage ever came as close at catching me off guard," Dom said, tugging a strand of her hair. "We have a long way to go and a lot more to learn about each other. I get that. But I need you, Avaline. Outside this room."

He cupped her chin and pinned her with his stormy eyes. "I won't share you though."

Avaline had no intention of sharing Dom either. But she had to go slow, especially around Henri's children. They would never believe her if she jumped into another relationship so soon. "I crave you like a drug, Dom. You've been under my skin for a long time now, and no matter how hard I tried to shelf it while I was dealing with life, and death, and restructuring my business—you were always there. And I always craved more.

"At the same time, I have to be sensible, especially out of respect for Henri and his children. I know it's unfair to ask, but can you wait for me again? I need time to sort all of this out fully. So I can start fresh with a clean conscience."

Dom sat up and pulled Avaline into his arms. "I've waited this long for you, Avaline. I'm not giving up on us—on you. Just promise me . . . no more White Room for personal use. It would kill me to think of you being with someone else after I've known your body this way."

He kissed her with the passion of a man in love. Claiming with his mouth what his heart could no longer deny. Dom was patient. He'd spent his life training with precision and patience to get the results he wanted. Waiting for Avaline was a no-brainer.

Avaline wrapped her arms around Dom's neck, running her fingers along the back of his scalp. "Have I ever told you how much I love your head?" she asked, grinning.

"Which one?" he teased back.

"Both," she admitted. "But I love your heart even more. I promise—I'm retiring the White Room for myself and am leaving it running in capable hands. I need to find myself again, Dom. Figure out who Avaline is without Henri and his legacy."

She brought her mouth to his, drawing his bottom lip in as she kissed him. Tingles shot through her body all the way to her toes and heated her tummy. It was different this time. This time, when their tongues curled and met in a moment of shared intimacy, it was no longer on borrowed time.

Avaline moaned as their kiss deepened, letting herself free-fall all the way into her future. This time, they had all the time in the world. This time, she had no intention of ever walking away from Dom again.

"Want me to call the owner?" Avaline whispered in Dom's ear. "I might be able to pull some strings so we can stay the night."

A heated look filled Dom's eyes. She knew that storm, and was ready to be consumed by it. "I might even try my hand at spanking," she teased.

It was all the encouragement he needed. Dom picked Avaline up and tossed her over his shoulder, heading toward the bedroom. He surprised Avaline when he opened a different set of doors off to the side. "It's about time we go back and revisit how we met, wouldn't you say?"

He set Avaline down on the shiny white boardroom table and placed his hands on either side of her. Dom leaned in for a kiss, taking her mouth in his and possessing every ounce of her being. This time, she wasn't running away from her life; she was creating a new one. And it never felt so good.

"But I'm the one who does the spanking," Dom said.

And so he did.

AFTERWORD

Thank you for reading *The White Room*. I hope you fell in love with the characters as much as I did. I loved them so much that I'm currently working on two spin-off series! In the meantime, you can find my other Kindle e-Books exclusively on Amazon:

Faith in Love—Sparks fly when philanthropist Egan MacGuire meets healer Celeste St. Angelo. Despite their painful pasts, can they find faith in love?

Proof of Love—When fate throws their stubborn hearts together, can Dez Wright & Mitch Michaelson move beyond their physical attraction to help those around them in need, all while searching for their own proof of love?

Last Night in Laguna—Bexley Rue has a gypsy soul. Kai Donovan wants nothing but love. Is one night together enough to heal her fractured life and tame her wild heart?

ABOUT THE AUTHOR

USA Today Best Selling Author C.M. Albert writes heartwarming romances that are both "sexy and flirty, sweet and dirty!" Her writing infuses a healthy blend of humor, inspiration, and romance. She's a sucker for a good villain, and a die-hard believer in everlasting love. In her spare time, she and her husband wrangle their two kids and enjoy spending time outdoors. When not writing or kid wrangling, C.M. Albert is also a Certified Medical Reiki Master, chocolate chip cookie aficionado, kindness ambassador, and seeker of naps. You can stay in touch with C.M. Albert or join her online at:

Website: www.colleenalbert.com

Amazon: www.amazon.com/C.M.-Albert

Facebook: www.facebook.com/cmalbertwrites

Colleen's Angels Street Team & Beta Reader Group:
www.facebook.com/groups/1015040795184238

Instagram: ww.instagram.com/cmalbertwrites

Twitter: www.twitter.com/colleenmalbert

Newsletter: http://eepurl.com/b6jIsz

Email: colleenalbert@icloud.com

LET'S TALK POETRY

Poetry has shaped the woman and writer I am today, so you will often see them referenced in my writing. One of my favorite poems of all times is "Nothing Gold Can Stay," which, admittedly, I first read as a teenager in *The Outsiders*, by S.E. Hinton. It stuck with me in a way few other poems have. This poem and the two others mentioned below are referenced briefly in the White Room because of my love for them. To learn more about poetry in general or to expand your horizons, visit the Poetry Foundation online. I hope the poems I mentioned touched you in some way. Poetry has a delicious way of sticking with you long after the poem has been read.

"Nothing Gold Can Stay," by Robert Frost
"I Like My Body When it is With Your," by e.e. cummings
"Twenty-One Love Poems [The Floating Poem, Unnumbered],"
by Adrienne Rich